IN BETWEEN BLINKS

BLINKS

A fairy tale for all ages

by J.L. Emmons

DEDICATION

Dedicated to my daughters, Tracy and Tammy, who I hope will always cherish the magic and mystery in life.

ACKNOWLEDGEMENTS

This book is a work of love and there are many people who I wish to acknowledge.

I joined a small writer's group in 2012 and it was there where I met Laura Henson and Rebecca Bauer. These two women helped me find my way and encouraged me to keep writing even when I felt like giving up. I wish to thank them for keeping my fire lit, giving me tips, and believing in me when I lost my way. I also would like to acknowledge and thank Mahala, another guiding force who helped me to search within myself for answers I didn't even know I needed.

A special thanks to my stepmother, Margaret Sjovold, who served as my sounding board when I felt like rambling, which was frequent. She allowed me to bounce ideas around regarding my numerous character changes and plot twists. Her support was a blessing, for sure.

And finally, I wish to thank my husband Dave Emmons, for allowing me the solitude to write. Distractions are an author's curse but my husband tried to keep them to a minimum. He listened to my ideas and shared in my enthusiasm.

Writing is more than sitting in front of a computer typing words. There are dreams. There are nightmares. There is research. There are the never-ending spell and grammar checks. No book will ever be perfect. At some point, you have to announce that it is finished and hope for the best. Thanks to everyone who allowed me to get to this point.

CHAPTER ONE

The forest was still asleep as young Sam sat up and stretched. The nights felt so long. After over a hundred years, give or take a few, Sam was still not used to the limbo that had become his existence. The long pauses, that time between nightfall and daylight were the hardest. Being a ghost was lonely.

The rabbits, birds, and deer that frequented the forest were Sam's entertainment. Sometimes he felt like they sensed him, that they knew he was there. He would get as close as possible hoping they wouldn't run away. He wanted to touch the forest animals but touching was no longer possible. Sam lost that ability when he died. His sense of smell still seemed to work. Seeing and hearing seemed enhanced, even better than when alive. Maybe he wasn't even speaking or the sounds were only in his head. So many questions. So much sadness.

Sam had never encountered another human ghost. Sometimes a young girl would visit the meadow near the lake. He didn't know who she was, but she seemed to be around his age, possibly eleven, or even twelve. She was taller than he was, but Sam knew boys don't catch up until their teens. He wished he'd had the chance to live into his teens.

The young girl brought her dog into the forest; a beautiful Collie named Sadie. The girl and Sadie swam in the lake and took walks through the woods. Sometimes she brought a picnic. Sam loved picnics. He liked to sit near the girl's blanket and watch as she pulled each item out of the basket and placed it next to her. The aroma seemed to waft towards him; the baked bread, the apple cider, and the fragrant cheese. Sadie wagged her tail and waited for a tossed piece of cheese or a fresh soft roll. Sometimes the dog gazed in his direction and tilted her head side to side.

"I died." There's that thought again. He couldn't shake it. Sam gazed at the early morning clouds, arms reaching out and shouted, "Where are you, Mama? Why can't I find you?" Sam slumped back down to the ground. He spoke out loud to the rabbit grazing not far away. "Little rabbit, can you see me?" The rabbit turned towards Sam then went back to eating.

Every day seemed like the next and the next. Sam often went to Willow Glen, a small town near the forest. He realized that he only had to think of where he wanted to go, and he'd be there. He discovered that he could also take a slower way and walk into town the way he used to. His imagined body still remembered walking, jumping, and skipping. Willow Glen was his home. He searched for his mother many times but everything looked so different now. Their cottage home was now occupied by another family. He felt more comfortable in the forest. He knew his mother was not in Willow Glen so there was little point in continuing his search there.

Sam looked around and saw trees, wildflowers, assorted mushrooms, and ferns. It was beautiful; this he could accept. It was the loneliness that was so hard to handle.

"Not much going on here," he mumbled, as he waved good-bye to a rabbit and focused his mind on the library in the middle of town.

§§§

"Watch out!" Sam shouted at the machine that ran right through him. The machines were horrible things. They rumbled, sputtered and splashed. Sam much preferred the horses and wagons. The horses seemed to sense where he was and walked around him. Drivers of the machines couldn't see him. Sam imagined throwing something at the loud rattling things.

The ghost boy climbed the steps to the library. He enjoyed watching his legs move. His mind could still give signals to his body to make it do the things it did when alive.

Sam didn't remember much about his childhood other than he lived with his mother in a small cottage. He worked in the stable while she worked in the big house. He didn't have a father, at least that's what his mother always told him. One day Sam grabbed a bucket to get grain for the horses. He took a shortcut and squeezed through a fence and pushed through some thick bushes. As he jumped past a bush, the ground gave way and he fell into a deep hole.

Sam remembered waking up but he felt different. He saw a small light in the distance but before he could move towards it, he found that he was out of the hole. He began to walk home but noticed his legs felt funny. He couldn't feel the ground beneath his feet. "What is happening?" he cried out. He couldn't see his house. "Help!" He tried calling but no one came. "Mama! I'm scared. Mama!"

Sam tried touching the tree next to him. His hand went right through it. He attempted to pick up a rock. He couldn't. It finally was clear to the frightened boy. He was dead.

"Where are the angels? If I'm dead, I'm supposed to go to heaven." Sam's thoughts seemed louder than usual. "What if I'm in hell? But it doesn't look like hell." The ghost boy slumped down and began his first day in the limbo that was now his existence.

§§§

The library was full this morning. Sam glanced over the shoulder of a young man seated at a table. The man brushed away a fly that wasn't there. That happened often when Sam was around.

People felt him but couldn't see him. He chuckled thinking that he must feel like a spider crawling down their faces.

There was a calendar on the wall. "Hey look. September 22. It's my birthday." Sam commented as he looked around. No one looked up. They continued pouring over their books and newspapers. "1912. Guess that would make me pretty old." He laughed but again, no one seemed to notice.

Sam thought back to his last birthday, his eleventh. It was September 22, 1805. That was over a hundred years ago. He knew his name was Samuel Charles Sullivan. Many things had changed in Willow Glen. His daily wishes were to find his mother and then, go to heaven. So far, he hadn't been able to do either.

CHAPTER TWO

Annie Harper blinked as the sun peaked through her bedroom window. Taking a moment to wake up, she realized it was Saturday. "No school. Sadie, we will have a picnic today." Annie pushed the slumbering collie off the bed. Sadie landed with a thud, not ready to wake in such a manner. The silky-haired dog stretched then rushed to the closed bedroom door.

"Yes, yes. I know. You need to go out." Annie grabbed her robe and slid her feet into her fleece-lined woolen slippers. Sadie bounded down the stairs and positioned herself in front of the door. "Get out of the way. How do you expect me to open this if you're sitting in front of it?" Annie pushed Sadie to the side and pulled open the large wooden door. Sadie ran outside, circled, sniffed, circled again and finally squatted to do her business.

This was their morning routine and the only way Annie's mother would allow Sadie to sleep upstairs. Annie knew that if Sadie had an indoor accident, the dog would be banished outside.

While waiting, Annie gazed out over her family's farm. Her father raised sheep and her mother sewed for neighbors and some of the townsfolk in Willow Glen. Annie loved how Sadie watched over the sheep. Collies were good sheepdogs and Sadie earned her keep.

"Feel better now?" Annie reached down and pet the head of her best friend. "Come on inside. I must get dressed. We have a busy day today."

The two went back into the cold, old farmhouse. Annie could smell bacon and eggs. Her mother was a great cook and Annie loved to eat. She had no siblings, at least not living ones. Her mother rarely talked about the three children that never made it past the age of six months. Annie was born after them. She was told she was a gift from heaven. Pampered and loved, she never felt wanting. A bit spoiled, she had her own room, her own dog, dolls, and beautiful clothes her mother made.

"Mama, breakfast smells delicious." The happy girl scooted up to the table.

"Thank you, sweetheart. We are waiting for your father. He'll be down in a minute." Manners were important to Mrs. Harper.

"I'm here. I'm here." Mr. Harper sat at the head of the table waiting for his wife to bring the plates to the table. "This looks delicious." Papa dug into his heaping plate of food. "This is a lot of food for one person. Are you trying to fatten me up?" Mr. Harper winked at his wife.

The Harper family discussed their plans for the day. "I'm going into town, Eileen. I have a buyer for our wool. Annie? Want to go with me? We could have a splendid day." Annie's father tapped Annie's nose, a loving gesture between the two of them.

"I was hoping to take a picnic to the forest with Sadie. May I go, please?" The young girl's eyes pleaded with her parents.

Mama glanced at Papa, "What do you think? Is she safe alone in the forest?"

"She'll be fine. She has Sadie and it's not like she hasn't roamed the forest alone before. Have fun but be home before dark." Papa tugged on one of Annie's brown braids, then winked. "You will be careful?"

"Yes, Papa. I will watch the sky and will come home long before it gets dark. I promise." Annie asked to be excused then prepared her picnic. Sadie's tail wagged at the sight of the basket. "Sadie, we will have such great fun."

"What are you doing today, Mama?" Annie asked. She knew her mother didn't like going with Papa when he was selling wool. Mama always thought the wool was worth so much more than the price they received.

"I thought about going to the library. Your father can take me on the way to the wool buyer." Mrs. Harper finished clearing the dishes.

"Would you please look for a book for me? One about dogs." Annie loved reading, especially books about animals.

"I will look and see what I can find. I'm sure there are many good choices. Are you sure you don't want to go with me?" Mrs. Harper asked.

"I'm sure. Sadie loves the forest so much. We will have a wonderful time." Annie's enthusiasm was hard to contain. She hadn't told anyone about the secret spot in the forest she had found.

The excited girl went upstairs to put on her play clothes. Her good clothes were for school and church, not for climbing trees or playing near the lake. She buttoned up her oldest frock and pulled on her scuffed boots. Annie was ready for any adventure that came her way.

Eileen and Joseph climbed into their wagon. Annie watched as the horses headed towards Willow Glen. "Don't forget. You are to be home before dark," Papa shouted from the seat.

Annie waved as they drove away then turned her attention to her prancing collie. "Sadie, are you ready?" Annie grabbed the picnic basket, a blanket, and made sure she had a coat this time. Even though the day was sunny, she didn't know what she would find inside the cave. It might be cold. Annie and Sadie followed the path towards the forest. The trail ran alongside a stone wall believed to be hundreds of years old. Annie wondered who had built such a sturdy wall. In England, there were many stories about how things had come to be. "Perhaps the druids or the Romans," she thought to herself. She then pictured herself in Roman attire, pulled down the road in a fancy chariot. Everyone told Annie that she had a vivid imagination. Since she had no siblings, her imagined adventures entertained her. She had no complaints. Annie loved the adventures she and Sadie experienced.

§§§

The walk to the forest took around thirty minutes. "This way Sadie," shouted the young girl, as she turned left at the third tree. The trail meandered through a maze of trees, but Annie knew exactly where to go.

The girl and excited dog reached a hill surrounded by bushes and vines. Annie pushed one large bush aside and a small dark hole appeared. It was too small for an adult to fit but large enough that Annie could squeeze through. "Here it is, Sadie. I knew I could find it again." The eager child pushed the basket into the hole. "Sadie, go in. I will be right behind you." The dog smelled the picnic basket and scurried into the hole. Annie wiggled through the opening as dirt fell onto her face and pebbles dug into her hands.

Once inside, the young girl realized she could see. There was enough room for her to stand up. Annie and Sadie made their way through the tunnel, around each curved wall. Annie watched for hanging spider webs. She noticed that on some of the walls, there were purple sparkly crystals embedded in the rock. The crystals seemed to be providing the light. As the duo meandered through the winding tunnel, Annie wondered if they were going to hit a dead end. Sadie sniffed the ground. Her tail wagged and her paws splashed in small puddles of water. "Maybe we should turn around, Sadie. I don't want us to get lost in here."

Annie was about to give up when the tunnel opened to a cavern. It was massive, about the size of three barns. More purple crystals were embedded in the cavern's walls. A large pool of water was in the center of the space and light was shining down from a hole at the top of the large space. There didn't seem to be a path around the pool, but Annie could see large, smooth rocks poking up from the water. They looked like stepping stones. Annie felt herself buzzing.

"Isn't it beautiful, Sadie? Look over there - fireflies." Annie moved closer to the specks of light that appeared to be zipping about through the air. As she got closer, she saw that they weren't fireflies at all. One landed on her nose. Annie attempted to wipe it away.

"Stop that," said a small voice.

"Who said that?" Annie turned around but saw no one.

"Are you blind? You almost squashed me." The sparkling light flew off Annie's nose.

Annie squinted and saw a hint of wings and a tiny face with tall pointed ears.

"Who are you?" Annie asked, not sure what she was seeing.

"I'm Phillip. You're trespassing," snapped Phillip.

Annie's eyes grew wide as she watched the speck of light grow larger and larger. A blue, winged creature stood before her. Phillip wore a blue tall pointed hat, short green pants, and a red and white striped shirt. Annie stepped back, frightened but also curious. Sadie barked, then jumped back and forth in front of the odd-looking being.

Phillip waved his hand towards the dog and Sadie calmed down. "No need to bark. Settle down. Settle down. I'm only a pixie." Sadie walked closer and sniffed him.

"What are you doing in my cave?" Phillip asked.

"Your cave? Why do you think it's yours?" Annie placed her hands on her hips and scowled.

"I've been living here much longer than you, small child. Shimmer belongs to the pixies. Do you realize what could happen to you for being here?"

13

"Shimmer? I never heard of a place called Shimmer." Annie showed no fear. How dare someone tell her she had no right to be in the cave.

"The pixies live here. It is our home and no one is allowed." Phillip pointed at Sadie. "What creature is this?"

"Creature? You mean Sadie?"

"It has long hair, a pointed nose, a tail, and four legs. It is not a troll, a fairy, a pixie, a dragon or a human." Phillip grabbed his chin, deep in thought. "Is it a horse? I have heard of those."

"You are a silly creature." Annie stared at Phillip. Can't you see it's a dog? Her name is Sadie."

"A dog? I have never seen this animal before. What does a dog do?"

"Dogs are companions. They play with us, sleep with us, protect us, and keep us company. Sadie is also a sheepdog. She helps my father round up the sheep on our farm without hurting them." Annie pulled Sadie closer, giving her a hug.

"Humans sleep with animals?" Phillip appeared shocked.

"Sadie is more than an animal. She's part of our family," Annie snapped back.

"Hmmm. I will have to observe your dog. The pixies from Shimmer don't often leave the cave. It is too dangerous. We have had bad experiences in the forests. It is much safer staying inside."

Annie didn't know what to think of Phillip. He was a magical creature who lived in a cave who didn't even know about dogs.

A grumble echoed through the cave. "What was that?" Phillip covered his ears.

Annie laughed. "That was my stomach silly. Haven't you ever heard a stomach growl before?"

"Growl? Do you have a troll inside of you?"

"Of course not. It's what stomachs do when they are hungry. I brought a picnic for me and Sadie. Would you like to join us?" Annie found a flat dry spot to spread out her blanket then sat down. She placed the crackers, cheese, and fruit onto a plate, then poured some apple juice into a cup. Sadie snuck a cracker.

Phillip sat down on the blanket. "I will try a berry."

Annie smiled and appreciated that Phillip was warming up to her. "Here, have a cracker. They taste wonderful with a piece of cheese."

Phillip took a small bite, then another. "This is delicious. Is this what you eat in your human land?"

"We eat many things, but this is our midday food. For supper, we often have lamb, rabbit, or venison stew."

With that comment, Phillip jumped back. "Meat? You eat meat? Oh my! You must leave immediately."

Annie jumped up and gathered her picnic items. "Why are you so angry?"

"Pixies do not eat meat. The deer and rabbits are our friends. How can you eat them? And you even sleep with them. Do they know you plan on eating them?" Phillip's face grimaced.

Annie was unsure of what to say. "Meat is important for us to stay healthy. I am sorry I offended you."

"How do I know you aren't planning to eat me?" Phillip kept backing away from the girl visitor.

"I have no intentions of eating you. Please, I'm sorry." Annie did not want to leave.

"You must assure me you will not eat our friends ever again."

"All right. I promise." Annie didn't know how she could keep that promise but for now, it seemed the right thing to say.

"So, tell me then, if you aren't here to eat us, why are you in our cave?" Phillip kept a safe distance.

"I didn't know it belonged to anyone. I found the entrance when Sadie chased a rabbit and it hopped into a bush. When I moved the bush, I found the hole. This is the first time I looked inside. It is so beautiful here."

"Usually, the alarm sounds when someone enters the cave. The crystal wind shuts down the tunnels so no one can get through. For some reason, no alarm sounded. Are you bewitched? How did you escape our alarm?" Phillip backed up.

"No, I'm not bewitched. What is this crystal wind?" Annie wondered why Phillip thought she was bewitched.

"There are forces here that you would not understand. The crystal wind comes from the purple crystals in the cave walls. They have special powers. They must've deemed you safe."

"Thank goodness. I am glad they let me enter," said Annie.

"The crystal wind has allowed you in so I must honor its decision. Please, tell me who you are. What is your name?" Phillip asked.

"Annie, my name is Annie Harper. I live on a farm outside of Willow Glen with my mother and father, Eileen and Joseph Harper."

"Pleased to meet you, Miss Annie Harper. Welcome to Shimmer. If you can stay awhile, I would like to introduce you to some of the others." Phillip relaxed and seemed more comfortable now.

"I would love that." Annie straightened her dress to be more presentable. She couldn't believe her good luck.

"I will be right back." Phillip changed back to firefly size and flew away.

While Annie waited, she gazed about the cavern. There seemed to be little windows of light, almost like small rooms. She wondered if the pixies lived in those little rooms. Her ears began ringing and a buzzing sound echoed through the cave. Annie looked to her right and saw a cloud of bright, little lights. The cloud moved closer and closer. One by one, the lights appeared along the side of the small lake. At first, they looked like orbs but then changed into looking more like Phillip. They had different sized noses and ears, different shapes of faces, and various colors of hats. All the pixies were blue.

"Annie, let me introduce you to some of my friends. This is Grayson. That fellow there is Sherman, and this is Lynnette. They are part of my pixie family. Since we are now acquainted, they will look out for you. We ask that you not tell anyone about our cave and please respect our rules."

"So nice to meet you all." Annie began shaking hands as each pixie approached. She noticed how delicate their fingers were. "Rules? What are your rules?"

"We do not hurt others. We do not bring anyone else here. We make ourselves available to our friends in times of need, and we do not eat meat."

"I can do that. I promise." Annie gave a reassuring nod to the pixies. They smiled as each one of the small beings stepped up in front of Annie and bowed.

"Pleased to meet you." Grayson removed his hat and performed a deep bow. "It is nice to meet you Ann-ee." Grayson sounded each syllable.

One by one, each pixie offered a greeting to the young girl who had drifted into their cave. Annie watched as each would become big and then change back into a small speck of light.

"How many pixies live here?" Annie asked.
Phillip grabbed his chin again, deep in thought. "Hmmm. I have never counted. A graction for sure."

Annie smiled at the sound of the funny word. "I guess a graction means a lot."

Phillip replied, "Of course," his face scrunched in confusion. "Everyone knows that."

"In that case, it appears I have made a graction of new friends. Thank you for letting me meet you all." Annie felt humbled.

"You are welcome but now I have work to do so will take my leave. Nice meeting you and your animal. I hope to see you again."

"Oh, I will be back. Sadie is the only one I bring to the forest. You should be safe. Are there any treats you like? I would love to bring you something special on my next visit."

"Pixies love treats, sweet treats." Phillip grinned. "Especially honey and berries. Might you have treats like those?"

"I will see you next time and yes, I will bring honey and berries. Good-bye Phillip." Annie waved as Phillip turned back into a tiny light and flew away.

"Sadie, guess we better go. We have been in the cave a long time." Sadie wagged her tail and scampered towards the cave door. Sadie squeezed through the hole with Annie right behind.

"Look Sadie. A crystal." Annie picked up the purple stone and placed it in her pocket. "I bet they won't mind. It will be nice having something special from this beautiful place. We better get home."

CHAPTER THREE

Annie skipped along the trail, pausing to pick up sticks now and then to throw for Sadie. Her dog loved to fetch, running to pick up the stick then refusing to drop it. "Let go. I can't throw it again if you don't drop it." The young girl pulled the stick out of the collie's mouth then threw it far down the trail.

The silky collie ran to pick up the stick and Annie chased after her. Annie pushed aside a fern and hopped over a moss-covered log.

"Hey, look out!" A voice shouted out.

Startled, Annie looked behind her. She saw a boy leaned up against the log she had jumped over. He seemed to be about her age, had shaggy brown hair and wore tattered clothes and a cap. His shoes looked old and scuffed.

"Hey sorry. I didn't see you there." Annie wondered who this strange boy could be.

The boy said nothing. He stared with his mouth wide open. "Who are you? I've never seen you before around here. Are you lost?" Annie walked closer to the boy who was now standing.

"You can see me?" asked the boy, his voice shaking.

"Of course, I can see you." Annie thought the question was strange.

"No one ever sees me, not in all the time I've been here." Sam appeared shocked.

"I've lived here a long time and I've never seen you before. Are you fibbing?" Annie wasn't sure she wanted to trust this scraggly-looking boy. He appeared hungry. She thought she should offer him something to eat.

"Are you hungry? I have some food in my basket." Annie set the basket down and took out some crackers and cheese.

"I can't eat but thank you just the same." Sam looked down at his feet.

"That's silly. You look hungry. Here, have a cracker." Annie walked closer to the boy and tried to place a cracker in his hand. She jumped back when she saw her hand go right through the boy's body. She dropped the basket and ran towards the path out of the forest.

"Wait! Don't be afraid. Please come back." Sam appeared next to her.

Annie stumbled and fell. "How did you get to me so fast?" She looked at the boy, terror written across her face. "What are you? Stay away from me."

"Please, don't be frightened. Please. Let me explain," Sam pleaded.

"Who are you?" Annie shouted.

"Sam, my name is Sam. I'm human like you, only not alive," replied the boy.

"What? What do you mean?" Annie's voice trembled.

"Don't be afraid. I'm not going to hurt you." The boy leaned over the shaking girl.

"Then you must be a ghost. But I don't believe in ghosts. How can I put my hand right through you?" Annie tried to make sense of the ghost boy.

"I'm a boy who happens to be dead. You are the first living person I've found who can see me," Sam remarked. "I've tried to find my mother. I seem to be stuck here."

"If you're dead, why aren't you in heaven?" Annie's voice shook.

"Been wondering the same thing myself." Sam reached for the girl but then remembered, he couldn't help her even if he wanted to. "I don't know why I didn't go to heaven. I want to find my mother even though she must be dead by now. I think I died over a hundred years ago."

"A hundred years? But you look my age." Annie's fear diminished. The boy didn't seem dangerous.

"I believe I'm eleven. That's how old I last remember being. I guess that's how it works when you're a ghost."

"How do I know you're not the devil?" Annie remembered what the pastor said about the devil and evil doers.

"I promise you; I am not the devil. I don't know how to convince you. But please give me a chance." Sam begged.

Annie stood up and brushed off the dirt and leaves. Sadie was no longer barking and instead was sniffing Sam's shoes.

"Please, I need your help. I want to find my mother. I know there must be information somewhere," said Sam.

"I might be able to help. What kind of information are you wanting?" Annie wondered how she might help.

"If I can find when she died or where she died, I am hoping I can connect with her spirit so she can help me get to heaven. I have waited so long." Sam appeared distraught.

Annie wanted to help the boy. "I bet we can find some information at the library, or the church. I will help you search." Her mind was already doing detective work, one of her favorite past times. She loved solving mysteries, like in the books she read.

"You will? Thank you. I am relieved you are not frightened. Not everyone would be willing to talk to a ghost." Sam's voice was much calmer now.

"You aren't scary. And you're only a boy. I'm not frightened at all. It will be nice to have someone to talk to. It's getting late. I need to get home."

"Too bad you can't travel the way I do. I only have to think of a place and I'm there," Sam said with a snicker.

"I have to walk with my legs so if you want to keep talking to me, guess you'll have to go the slow way." Annie picked up her basket and turned to leave. "When we get to my house, I'm not sure how my family will react to you."

"They won't be able to see me. I still don't know how you can. Do you have special powers?" Sam tugged on his cap.

"I don't know. I have been to this forest many times and I've never seen or heard you." Annie kept walking.

"Have you done anything different this visit to the forest? I have seen you many times before, but you never noticed me." Sam tried to touch Annie, but his hand went right through her.

Annie pondered everything that was different. She couldn't tell Sam about the cave. She had made a promise to Phillip. The basket was nothing new and the food wasn't unusual. Her clothes were the same. She reached inside her pockets and felt the purple crystal. She pulled it out and held it in her hand for Sam to see. "This is the only thing different. I found it today and decided to take it home with me."

Sam stared at the faceted stone. "It is making me dizzy."

"That must be it!" Annie smiled.

"The crystal must give you special abilities to see ghosts," Sam said.

Annie turned the crystal over in her hand. She didn't feel anything unusual. "Let's try something. What if I put the crystal over there on that log and then see what happens?" She walked past three large trees and placed the crystal on a mossy log. She turned to walk back and noticed Sam was gone. "Where did you go?" There was no reply. Gazing about, she saw no one and heard nothing.

"Sadie, do you see Sam?" Sadie ran around in a circle and barked. Annie turned back and picked up the crystal. She looked at

Sadie and there was Sam, right next to where Sadie circled. "This has to be it. It's the crystal that allows me to see you and hear you. It looks like Sadie can see you even without the crystal." Annie could hardly contain herself after discovering the secret.

"That is curious. Where did you find it?" Sam asked.

"Along the path." She couldn't tell him the truth. She had promised Phillip.

"Is it bewitched? How else could it work?" Sam seemed relieved.

"Bewitched? Isn't that a bad thing?" Annie worried now that she shouldn't be holding the crystal.

"I'm not sure. For now, it's a good thing," Sam said with a smile.

"Now that we know, I guess I will need to carry this with me all the time, at least if I want to be able to see you." Annie put the purple stone back in her pocket.

The trio headed towards the farm. Annie felt buzzy, as if magic stirred around her. She hoped her parents couldn't see Sam. It would be too hard to explain who he was. Annie knew that something special was happening. She felt odd. The buzziness was not going away. Sadie pranced in front of her. If Sadie wasn't afraid, it must be alright.

CHAPTER FOUR

Joseph urged Rosie, their old brown mare towards the barn. She was a good horse and had served the family a long time. He took off the harness and put the wagon into the covered shelter. Joseph then went back to Rosie and led her into her stall. He loved brushing her down, thinking about all the trips they had made. The sweaty smell of horse hair mingled with the scent of fresh oats warmed Joseph's heart. He was a lucky man, married to the love of his life Eileen and raising his beautiful daughter Annie.

"I'll be right in to wash up," Joseph yelled out to Eileen, who was standing on the porch. He removed his boots before entering the house, one of his wife's strict rules.

"I wondered how much longer you were going to be. I already have supper started," Eileen said with a snippy tone.

"Everything alright?" Joseph asked.

"I'm a little tired. I thought Annie would be home by now," Mrs. Harper said.

"What a day. Frank paid me a good price for the wool. We should be comfortable this winter. You can buy that fabric you've been eyeing at the mercantile and there is enough money to stock up the pantry. How was the library?" Joseph changed the subject.

"I saw a few friends and I found some books for Annie. I know you prefer doing your business without having your wife in the way. Our library is a good place for me to catch up on the latest news," Eileen said, with a slight smile.

"You could have come with me even though I know talking shop isn't your favorite thing to do," said Joseph, as he winked at his pretty wife. "At least the library is a nice place to spend the day."

Eileen's eyes showed worry. She gazed out the window. "Annie and Sadie aren't home. It's getting late." She untied a stack of books and placed two on the table. "I hope Annie hasn't read these yet."

"She's eleven, old enough to be careful, plus she has Sadie. They probably lost track of time." Joseph opened the back door, put his boots back on, and walked towards the barn. He knew how his wife worried but Annie could be trusted. She was a smart girl and he'd taught her many things about staying safe in the forest. They weren't in the barn so he walked towards the woods. In the distance, he saw Annie and her dog. He didn't want his daughter to think he was checking up on her so he turned back before she saw him.

"They're coming. Almost home as a matter of fact." Joseph heard his wife's sigh of relief, coupled with a few quick sobs. This wasn't the first time Eileen had reacted this way.

Joseph knew why his wife worried. Eileen thought something terrible would happen to their beautiful daughter. They had already lost three infants to a rare disease. The doctors said there should be no more births. It was too hard on Eileen and had taken an emotional and physical toll. She could not handle the deaths of anymore children. They both had wanted a large family, but it wasn't meant to be. Some friends suggested the orphanage in Penzance, about an hour's ride.

§§§

Mr. Harper remembered the day in detail. Five years ago, he and Eileen walked into the large, gray four-story building in Penzance. Their hopes were high and their hearts full. The orphanage looked like any other building. Joseph knew there were many children inside and he wondered how many of them would never find homes.

He helped Eileen climb down and looked up at the large wooden door. Would they find a child inside, to love? What if it wasn't meant to be? What if they weren't meant to have a family?

"We must keep an open mind. Girl or boy, it doesn't matter. We will know the right one when we meet." Joseph wanted to believe the words he spoke to his wife.

"Yes dear. Girl or boy. Or maybe both," Eileen replied, her nervous hands shaking.

Joseph knocked on the door and waited. It seemed like a long time before a short middle-aged woman opened the door. Before he had a chance to speak, the woman invited them inside.

"Good day. I assume you are here to see the children. I'm Mrs. Johnson, one of the caretakers.   Let me show you to the parlor."

"Yes, we mailed a letter to you. We are the Harpers, Joseph and Eileen. We have not been blessed with children and have come to see if there may be a special child for us." Joseph winced as Eileen squeezed his hand a bit too hard. "I correct myself. We had three children who died very young. My wife's physician said it would be unhealthy for her to have another."

"Oh, I see. I am so sorry for your loss. Let's hope there will be a child here who will be to your liking." Mrs. Johnson motioned towards a settee. "Please sit down and make yourselves comfortable. I will prepare some tea and then we will talk."

"Tea would be lovely. Thank you, Mrs. Johnson," said Eileen.

"I expected to see children everywhere. Where do you think they are?" Joseph asked, his eyes scanning the large room.

"It's a beautiful day. They must be outdoors playing." Eileen approached the window. "Yes, see? There they are, playing in the yard."

"After we have tea, we'll go outside and watch them play." Joseph imagined children on swings and slides.

Eileen walked back to the settee. "There are so many children, Joseph. How will we ever decide?"

"Here we are. I brought some biscuits." Mrs. Johnson poured the tea and sat on a chair near the couple. "So tell me, what age of child are you looking for?"

Mrs. Harper looked at her husband, then to Mrs. Johnson. "Age is of no concern. We want a child, one who needs us and who wants to be part of our family."

"There are plenty here who would qualify. They are all playing outside, except our little Annie. She prefers to read. She isn't like the others." The woman smiled.

"May we meet this girl, this Annie?" Joseph asked.

"Why of course. Let me find her. She is usually in the library. I must warn you, Annie is not like other children. She keeps to herself and isn't very talkative." Mrs. Johnson left to fetch Annie.

Eileen turned to her husband. "What about the children outside? Don't you want to see them? A boy might be helpful with caring for the sheep."

"A girl could be helpful for you in the kitchen, and then who says that a girl can't help with sheep? Besides, I have a feeling about this little girl. I'm not sure why, but I think she may be the one for us. Let's see how we get along with Annie. If it doesn't go well, we will go outside and observe the others." Joseph put his arm around his wife then reached for a biscuit. "Try one of these. Delicious."

"How can you eat at a time like this?" Eileen scolded.

With a slight chuckle, Joseph pushed the entire biscuit into his mouth. Mrs. Johnson entered the room with a lovely young girl with long brown braids. He tried to smile but his mouth was full. He wondered what the girl must think.

"Mr. and Mrs. Harper, this is Annie. Annie, these are the Harpers. They wanted to meet you." Mrs. Johnson guided the shy child closer to the Harpers.

"Delighted to meet you Annie." Joseph held out his hand.

"Pleased to make your acquaintance." The young girl curtsied then shook Joseph's hand.

"You are a beautiful girl. I love your pretty brown braids. Look. Your hair is the same color as mine." Eileen touched her own hair then reached out her hand.

"Thank you, ma'am. Your hair is nice too," said Annie with a polite smile.

"How old are you, Annie?" Mrs. Harper asked.

"I just turned six," the girl replied, her shyness diminishing.

"Six? Mrs. Johnson said you are good at reading, quite an accomplishment for someone only six," Eileen commented. "What else do you like to do besides reading?" Eileen asked.

"I love to draw, and I especially like to play with the animals." Annie's face lit up.

"That's wonderful. We have many books and we also have a farm with sheep. Do you like sheep?" Joseph asked.

"Oh yes sir. I love sheep. They are soft and squishy and they have funny voices."

"I guess you could call their baa-baa sound, a voice," said Joseph with a chuckle. "What else do you like to do?"

"I like to sleep because I love my dreams," said Annie.

"What kind of dreams do you have?" asked Eileen.

"I dream that I can fly. Sometimes I can fly over the trees like the birds. When I wake up, I remember the places I saw."

'That sounds wonderful. I wish I could remember my dreams. Do you like to play with the other children?" Mrs. Harper asked.

"They don't like me very much. They think the fairies stole me because I was found in a forest. They call me names and throw sticks at me." Annie looked down at her shoes. "I like to keep to myself."

"Is this true?" Joseph flashed a scornful look at Mrs. Johnson.

"It is true that Annie was found in the forest by some hunters. She was very young. No one knows where she came from or who her parents were. The hunters brought her here. She's been with us ever since. And yes, the other children do tease her often because she isn't like them. We don't know her real birthday so we celebrate it on the date she arrived here. We guessed her age."

"And you allow the other children to tease this poor child? Has no one inquired about her?" Joseph asked, his tone already protective of the young girl.

"We can't watch the children every second and we have scolded them. It doesn't seem to matter. That's one reason we allow Annie to stay inside. No one has inquired about her. Most couples who want to adopt want either an infant or they want a sturdy boy who can help with the farm work. Very few want the girls."

"Annie, I am so sorry that you get teased. You are a lovely girl and considering you love to read, you must be very smart." Eileen peered into the young child's face.

"I know many words and I can write, too. The other children here don't like to study. But I do. Look, I am learning about the stars." Annie opened the book to an illustration showing stars and planets in a dark blue sky.

"That's wonderful," said Eileen. "What other things do you like?

"I love picnics. Oh, and I love chocolate. And, of course, I love the flowers and the trees and the lakes and the rivers. I love everything," said Annie, her voice filled with passion.

Eileen smiled at Joseph and squeezed his hand. That was the only sign he needed to know that they had found their child.

"Mrs. Johnson, might we talk to you in private?" Joseph whispered.

"Annie, why don't you go upstairs and get your art book. The Harpers might enjoy seeing some of your drawings." Mrs. Johnson waited until the girl was out of sight.

"We know it's sudden, but we would like to take Annie home with us. What do we need to do to adopt her?" Joseph's eyes pleaded.

"Are you sure? We usually allow the child a month or two of visits before reaching a decision. We want to make sure that both the child and the parents are a good fit." The woman seemed surprised.

"We don't need months to decide. We have already lost three children to an unfortunate disease. We want a family and Annie seems perfect," remarked Eileen, her voice shaking with emotion.

"I can see that you are serious," commented Mrs. Johnson. "Annie loves animals. I'm sure she would love your farm."

"We have many animals on the farm. We could even get her a dog." Joseph knew of some collie puppies that had recently been born.

"It appears this is settled then. I have some papers you will need to sign but first, I'd like to ask Annie," said Mrs. Johnson. "Here she comes. Please look at her art. She loves to draw."

Annie placed her art book on the table. She flipped through the pages. There were sketches of the stars, trees, animals, and flowers.

"You are an excellent artist. These drawings are wonderful. What is this one about?" Eileen paused at a drawing of a forest with a colorful rainbow next to a large tree. There was a door in the tree.

"I imagine that this is the forest where the hunters found me. Over here is the door. See it?" Annie pointed to the small door in the tree trunk.

"Very nice," said Eileen, as she gazed at Annie's drawing.

"Thank you," Annie replied.

"Who lives behind the door?" Eileen asked.

"Why the fairies of course," remarked Annie, her face serious.

Annie turned the page to the next drawing. "These are my stones. They're crystals."

"Those are lovely. Do you like stones?" Eileen asked.

"I love stones. I used to have so many, but they went missing. That's why I draw pictures of them. I love the purple ones the most." Annie continued turning the pages.

Joseph realized how bright this girl was and with a healthy imagination. "Has she always been like this?"

Mrs. Johnson replied, "Yes indeed. Like I said, she is unlike the other children."

Eileen reached for Annie's hand. "Annie, do you like living here?"

"It's all right. I wish I could have a dog though. Pets aren't allowed here." Annie closed her sketchbook.

The Harpers looked at each other with the same look. There was no question they both wanted the same thing.

"Would you like to come live with us? You would make a lovely daughter." Joseph reached out to hug the young child, not knowing if she would resist. Annie fell into his arms and hugged him. Eileen joined in the hug and it was at that moment, Joseph knew they finally had a family.

31

§§§

Now here it was, five years later, and Annie had been the answer to their prayers. Joseph and Eileen promised each other they would let their daughter's imagination soar. Annie loved spending time in the forest with her dog Sadie. The collie was the perfect companion for a child who wanted to be outside more than inside.

Eileen was so happy. Joseph did his best to protect his wife and daughter but Annie's explorations often caused worry. He was glad Annie had Sadie with her but now and then, something seemed off. He couldn't explain it.

Eileen wiped her stressed damp hands on her apron. "I will start supper and will call you when it's ready."

Joseph saw the strain on his wife's face. He didn't know how to help her relax, to enjoy being a mother. His wife was so fearful of losing another child, she fretted over every little thing. No wonder their daughter liked spending so much time alone in the forest.

Eileen had already started supper when Annie bounded into the house. Joseph turned and saw his daughter's red and windblown face. He then heard his wife's muffled sigh, a sigh of relief.

"We had the most wonderful time. I even found a beautiful purple stone along the path. Mama, do you have some cord and wire I could use so I can wear it around my neck?" Annie held up the sparkly crystal.

"That's beautiful. I have the perfect thing." Eileen's face relaxed. "I'm glad you're home. It was getting late."

"Sorry Mama. We lost track of time. Come on Sadie. Let's go get cleaned up for supper." The pair headed upstairs.

Joseph went to his wife and wrapped his arms around her. "You can't keep doing this. Annie is growing up. Before long, she'll be moving away and starting her own family. We must learn to let go. We will always be a family but there will come a time when she will leave us."

CHAPTER FIVE

Sam looked around the room. He had followed Annie upstairs knowing her parents couldn't see him. "So, what's this?" He pointed to a wooden box on the chest of drawers.

"That's a radio? Haven't you seen one before?" Annie turned it on. "See? It plays music and there are radio shows and comedy hour and the news. My parents bought it for me on my last birthday. It was very expensive."

Sadie turned up the sound and Sam jumped. "Who's in there? A voice is coming from inside. Is it sorcery?"

"Of course not. It uses electricity. See?" Annie pointed to the cord and where it plugged into the wall. "It works through that cord."

"Electricity? What's that?" This was too much for Sam to understand. He often went to the library but had never seen a radio. He imagined there were many things that were part of this new world. So much had changed.

Sam wandered around. "I like your room. It looks very comfortable. You sure have a lot of dolls." Sam gazed into the eyes of a very large doll that looked lifelike. He tried to poke it but his finger went right through her porcelain head.

"That's Elizabeth. She's my favorite doll. My parents gave her to me on my seventh birthday." Annie straightened the doll's pinafore and smoothed down the brown braids. "...and this is Penny. She's the one I sleep with."

Sam laughed when he saw a ragged looking doll that was missing hair and only had one eye. "What happened to her?"

"Sadie pulled off one of the eyes. I never did find it. Papa said Sadie probably pooped it out by now," said Annie, her face crinkled in disgust.

"That's funny. Bet you wouldn't want it even if you found it," said Sam, laughing as he imagined the dog pooping out a glass eyeball.

"Mama says Penny has been with me since I came here. I guess I love her too hard. That's why she doesn't have much hair left." Annie placed Penny back on the bed.

"What do you mean since you came here? Where were you before?"

"The orphanage; the one in Penzance. My parents picked me out special," Annie commented with a smile.

"So, you're an orphan? What happened to your real parents?" Sam seemed surprised but then realized that Annie didn't have her parents either.

"Mama and Papa 'are' my real parents," Annie replied sternly.

"I mean your birthparents. What happened to them?" Sam's curiosity grew. He had never met an orphan before but figured it wasn't as bad as being a ghost.

"I know nothing about them; only what I was told at the orphanage. Someone found me in the forest. I was very young. My new Mama and Papa picked me out when I was around six, although no one knows my real birthday."

"You don't even know when your birthday is?" Sam felt bad for his new friend.

Sam quit asking orphan questions and instead focused on the items in Annie's room. "I like your drawings. I used to like to draw. What's in this one?" Sam pointed at one that showed tiny people with wings.

"Those are my dream people. They fly and their wings shimmer." Annie gazed at her drawing. "...and see that little door in the tree? That's how I get inside to their lands."

"You have an interesting imagination. Do they talk to you?" Sam figured Annie was telling a story, and not even a believable one.

"Of course they do. They like to tell me that they are always near and that they are happy I have such nice parents. They also tell me I'm loved and to enjoy my life. It's a nice dream." Annie stared at the drawing, her mind far away in thought.

"At least you are loved, even in your dreams. You are very lucky." Sam bowed his head. He wondered if anyone loved him.

"Yes, I suppose. Sometimes Mama worries about me too much, though. Papa says I need to be more careful so I don't make Mama worry." Sam could tell that Annie wasn't always happy.

"She must love you very much. I wonder if my mother ever worried about me?" Sam wondered about many things, but most of all, about his mother. He wondered if she looked for him or if she knew he was a ghost. Did she know that he hadn't gone to heaven? He wondered if she lived a long life or if she died young. All the things Sam had been told about heaven, never happened.

"I need to get cleaned up. I know you don't eat so if you want, you can stay in my room. I can get some books out for you." Annie tied bows onto her long brown braids.

Sam wished he could touch Annie's hair, to feel it like a living person could feel. He then thought about Annie's room. There was so much to see. "Books are great if someone can turn the pages for me. What I'd really like is for you to let me listen to your radio." Sam moved closer to the box.

"Wonderful idea. I will turn it to something I think you would like." Annie turned the dial back and forth, the static buzzing and crackling until she found the radio mystery show. She tuned the radio until the sound was loud and clear. "This is a show I like. It might be scary. It's like a play, except you only get to hear their voices."

"Not much scares me, so yes, I will listen to that." Sam settled onto Annie's bed. "Wish I could feel this bed. Bet it's soft."

"It's very soft. My Papa ordered it for me, special." Annie smiled at Sam and then buckled her shoes. "Make room for Sadie. You're in her spot."

At the mention of her name, Sadie lurched up onto the bed, almost landing on top of Sam. "I guess we can share." The dog seemed to gaze at Sam then put her head down. Sam loved animals. He was glad that Sadie didn't growl at him like some of the animals in the forest. "It seems like Sadie can see me."

"She saw you in the forest so I imagine she can still see you now. She usually stays up here while I eat because Mama doesn't like it when Sadie begs at the table. Mama knows that Papa gives Sadie food under the table, so I must keep her upstairs. At least she can keep you company." Annie closed the door behind her and headed downstairs for supper, leaving the radio on for Sam.

Sam gazed around the room, trying to remember how it felt to be alive. He couldn't touch, taste, or smell anything. He heard Sadie snoring. A voice echoed from the radio.

'Don't go in there. There is a killer on the loose.'
'But my husband is in there. I know he's in there.'
'Ma'am. If your husband is in there, he's a goner. All the patrons have been shot.'
Music plays. Shots are fired.
'He's coming back. Look out!'
A woman screams.
'And now, a word from our sponsor.'

Sam listened to a woman talking about soap. There was more music and then some high-pitched sounds coming from the box. Soon, the radio show's voice again came out of the box.
'Thank you for tuning in to The Mystery Hour. We now return you to our story.'
'Out of my way or I will shoot you too.'
'You killed my husband. I won't let you get away with this.'
Music plays. People are heard struggling, fighting. A man yells.
'You stabbed me.'
A body falls. A woman can be heard crying.
'What will I do now? I killed him.'
Sirens are heard. More music plays.
'Stay tuned for the next episode of The Mystery Hour.'
The radio crackles and another voice echoes from the box.
'Thank you for listening to The Mystery Hour. Please tune in again tomorrow at this same time. Have a good evening'.

Sam was disappointed that the radio show ended. He thought it was great that he could listen to a mystery instead of having to read. He would ask Annie to find another radio story for him to enjoy after her supper. His curiosity became too much and the young boy looked around Annie's room. There were so many books on the shelves, small figurines, dolls, and a jar full of marbles. He wished he could take the marbles out of the jar and play with them. He was overcome by a feeling of loneliness. Even though Annie could see him, he was still dead, and he still had no idea of how to find his mother or how to get to heaven.

"Hey Sadie. Guess it's just you and me." Sam stroked Sadie's head and Sadie appeared to feel Sam's hand.

CHAPTER SIX

"I'm hungry." Annie pulled her chair out from the table. "Sadie is sleeping upstairs. I think I wore her out, but we had a lot of fun today." Annie kept thinking about the crystal she had found, the cave, and meeting all the pixies. But she especially was thinking about Sam. How was she going to tell her parents about the boy in her room, or even worse, the 'ghost' boy in her room?

"I made a special treat for dessert. I know you both love apple pie." Mrs. Harper removed her apron and sat down at the table. She ladled chunks of meat, carrots, and potatoes, onto plates and placed them in front of Annie and Papa.

Mr. Harper winked at his daughter then glanced at Mrs. Harper. "Delicious sweetheart. I always knew I married the best cook in the county."

Annie made sure her napkin was in her lap so she could protect her dress. She spooned up a bite and held it under her nose, smelling the pungent aroma of mutton. Annie thought of Phillip and the promise she had made. "Mama? I don't want to eat meat any longer. I don't have much of an appetite for it." Annie forced tears from her eyes. "Those poor animals."

"Why Annie, you have always loved my stews. You said lamb stew was your favorite," Mrs. Harper remarked.

"I know Mama, but I don't want to eat meat anymore. Please don't make me," Annie pleaded. She made the saddest face she could manage.

"You need to eat meat to be healthy," Mama said with concern.

"I'm not going to change my mind." Annie pushed her chair away from the table, crossed her arms across her chest, and pouted.

"Annie, your mother is right. You need to eat meat. You are not getting up from the table until you finish your stew," said Mr. Harper, his voice sharp and stern. "A face like that will send you to bed without any supper at all, and no apple pie."

Mrs. Harper looked at her husband. "Annie is old enough to decide what she wants to eat. When she gets hungry enough, she will change her mind."

"But in this house, there are rules. My rule is that Annie eats what she is served. End of discussion." Annie's father glared down at his bowl.

The family ate in silence, not something they usually did. Annie ate all the vegetables in her bowl but moved the meat to the side. She hoped her father wouldn't notice. She also ate a biscuit, some apple slices, and some cheese. She wished she could be upstairs with the ghost boy. "May I be excused?" Annie asked.

"As soon as you finish that meat in your bowl," Papa replied.

"But Papa, I can't. I just can't," shouted Annie as she burst into tears.

"May I see you in the kitchen?" Mrs. Harper motioned to her husband.

The Harpers left the table and walked into the kitchen. Annie could hear her parents shouting. She heard a pan slam against the counter and she heard them arguing.

"What's wrong with you?" Annie heard her father yell. "Why are you coddling that girl? Rules are rules."

Annie heard her mother say, "I am going to tell her she doesn't have to eat anything she doesn't want to."

Joseph stormed out of the house, slamming the door. Eileen came back to the table and sat down. Annie could see that her mother was upset.

"Annie, sweetheart. You don't have to eat anything you don't want to. Your reasons are your reasons and you are entitled to them. Here, let me take that bowl away. Your father won't be coming back to the table," said Mrs. Harper, her hands visibly shaking.

Concerned, Annie reached for her mother's hand. "I'm sorry, Mama. I didn't mean for you and Papa to argue."

"Why don't you go upstairs and listen to your radio before bed. Your father will calm down. Don't worry. I will save the pie for tomorrow. I don't think anyone feels like dessert tonight," said Mrs. Harper, her sadness evident.

"Thank you, Mama." Annie pushed herself away from the table and headed upstairs.

§§§

"My parents are fighting." Annie sat down on her bed.

"What are they fighting about?" Sam asked. He had the impression Annie's parents were perfect. It surprised him to hear that they were angry.

"I told them I didn't want to eat meat anymore. My father got upset."

"Why don't you want to eat meat?" Sam looked puzzled. He remembered back when he could eat. "Humans are supposed to eat meat."

"I decided. That's all," Annie snapped at Sam.

"But you live on a sheep farm. That's what sheep farmers do. They raise sheep for wool, milk, cheese, and meat. People need these things," said Sam, as he reasoned with the girl. She was confused, for sure.

"The wool, milk, and cheese are fine. That's not hurting anything. But killing an animal to eat it? No. It's wrong and sad," Annie said sternly.

"I'd give anything to be able to eat again, a nice juicy pork chop or some fried chicken. You don't know how lucky you are," said Sam, describing the meals he used to enjoy.

"You can have your opinion, but I don't want to eat meat any longer. And that includes birds, too. Can we talk about something else?" The girl sounded serious.

"Your choice little lady. Why don't we talk about the radio?" Sam loved listening to it and wanted to know more about it.

"Sure. What did you think about the mystery show?" Annie asked.

"It was amazing, except it stopped before it solved the mystery. They said to stay tuned until tomorrow. Why do I have to wait until tomorrow to find out how it ends?" Sam didn't understand why they hadn't told the whole story. The mystery was left unfinished.

"It may not even end tomorrow. Sometimes the mysteries go on for weeks. That's how they get you to keep listening," said Annie with a giggle. "Where do you go at night, Sam? Do you sleep?" Annie asked.

"I don't sleep. I usually curl up somewhere because everything gets dark. I listen to sounds, and my thoughts. It gets pretty boring and lonely." Sam thought about the endless nights. If only he could sleep again. He missed so many things.

"How sad for you. I would offer to leave the radio on, but the station ends at ten o'clock. It doesn't come back on until 6:00 tomorrow morning," Annie remarked.

"I'll curl up next to Sadie. She doesn't seem to mind me being close to her. It seems like she actually can feel me." Sam snuggled up next to the sleeping dog, even though he couldn't feel the fur or the body, he was sure was warm and soft.

"Turn around so I can change my clothes." Annie hid behind her bed and slipped on her nightgown. "There, I'm done."

"I wasn't going to look," Sam wondered why Annie wanted to hide. He had seen girls before, and besides, what difference did it make? He was a ghost boy.

"I wanted to make sure," said Annie, her cheeks blushing pink. "I'm going to read for a while. That's what I usually do before I go to sleep. Do you want to read with me?" Annie climbed into bed and reached for the book on her nightstand.

"I would like that very much." Sam perched himself closer to Annie so he could read the pages. He noticed that Annie turned the pages before he could finish, but that was okay. He wasn't paying attention anyway. So much had happened that now, he only wanted to enjoy having someone to talk to, someone who could hear him.

Annie closed the book and reached for her light. "Good night Sam."

"Good-night, Annie." Sam went to the window and sat in the chair, gazing at the full moon. Nights were long. Sometimes he would count stars. Sometimes he would sing songs. Even though he had a new friend, he was still a ghost.

CHAPTER SEVEN

Annie struggled to make sense of the sound. "What is that?" Her mind wasn't functioning yet. "Oh, that darn bird." Annie realized it was the rooster waking up the farm.

She stretched, rubbed the sleep from her eyes, and looked towards the door for Sadie. As expected, Sadie was waiting to go out for her daily duty. Annie got out of bed, put on her slippers, then remembered the crystal hanging around her neck.

"Sam." She looked around the room, but the ghost boy was nowhere in sight.

"Let's go Sadie." The dog and girl bounded down the stairs, their routine well established. Sadie ran out the door and began to circle, looking for the perfect spot to handle nature's call. Annie could see Sam now. He was standing outside gazing towards the barn. "Sam. There you are." Annie walked towards him and then remembered she only had on slippers. Sam immediately was standing next to her.

"How did you do that? You were way over by the barn." Annie was curious about all the things Sam could do.

"I could tell you wanted to talk to me, so here I am," said Sam, a large grin across his face.

"You can move that fast?" Annie was still surprised by this whole ghost thing.

"As fast as a blink of an eye," Sam replied.

"I need to tell my parents about you. They can help you find out some answers." Annie wondered how they'd take it.

"Do you think that's a good idea? Why would they believe in a ghost boy? I think you should keep it a secret," said Sam, quite concerned.

44

"Guess we won't know until we try." They all went back into the house, Sadie's tail bouncing with each step. Mr. and Mrs. Harper were sitting at the table in the kitchen.

"Papa, I'm sorry about last night. I hope you're not still angry." Annie walked up to her father and kissed him on the cheek.

"I'm not angry. I don't like that you don't want to eat meat anymore. I've talked to your Mama and she believes you're old enough to make your own decisions. From now on, realize that you will need to prepare your own supper. Your Mama should not have to make two separate meals."

"I understand. I know how to cook. Mama has taught me many recipes. I even know how to bake bread," said Annie, her face beaming. Her mother had shown her how to prepare the yeast and how to knead. Sometimes Mama helped when the dough was too thick. Annie's hands were still small. "I can bake cookies too."
"Cookies. Now that's a splendid idea," remarked Papa as he rubbed his stomach.

"Today we need to bake," Eileen spoke up.
"Sure Mama. We can do that. But first, there's something I'd like to tell you."

"Is something wrong?" Eileen asked.

"No, nothing's wrong. When I was in the forest yesterday, uh, I need to tell you that I met someone, a boy," Annie stammered. She was nervous and it showed.

Joseph smiled then winked at his wife. "A boy, huh?"

Annie could tell that her father thought something else. "No Papa. It's not like that. He's not just any boy."

"Of course not," Mr. Harper chuckled, then winked again.
Annie was not liking her father's teasing. "Mama, Papa, I met a boy who is over a hundred years old." She waited for their reaction.

"What? You're joking, aren't you?" Papa's look changed.

"What do you mean, Annie? How can a boy be over a hundred years old?" Mrs. Harper grinned.

"Sadie and I were running through the forest and I jumped over a log. I heard someone shout at me and noticed a boy behind the log. I almost landed on him. Sadie was barking and the boy was surprised that I could see him," said Annie as she relayed the story. She knew it sounded absurd.

"Why would he think you couldn't see him?" Mama asked.

"Because he's a ghost." Annie noticed the silent stare of her parents. "Aren't you going to say anything?"

"Annie, are you feeling alright? You know there's no such things as ghosts," Papa announced.

"I'm fine and yes, I know that's what everyone thinks, but he's real. He's here right now." Annie pointed to the chair where Sam sat. He was holding up his hands in a shrug to show Annie he was right. They weren't going to believe her.

The Harpers looked to where Annie was pointing. "Why yes, we see him. A young boy, sitting right over there." Mrs. Harper pointed.

"Oh yes, of course, a fine-looking lad." Joseph winked at Eileen.

"You don't believe me." Annie could tell they were teasing her. She then remembered the crystal. "Here. Hold this and then look." Annie handed the crystal to her mother knowing the stone had special powers.

"Sweetheart, it's nice you have an imaginary friend. Make sure you take Sadie with you when you go into the forest." Eileen handed the stone back to Annie. "Now get ready for breakfast and then when we're finished, we can bake some bread."

Annie put the crystal around her neck and stomped out of the kitchen. Sam was right next to her. "They couldn't see you Sam. How come the crystal didn't work?" Annie was upset.

"Maybe it only works for you? I don't know. I guess your parents aren't going to be helping us, but it's better this way." Sam seemed relieved.

"But they'd know where we could look," Annie commented. The information Sam needed was going to be hard to find. Her parents could've helped.

"I already know where we can look. The library has lots of information but I need someone who can turn the pages," Sam said.

"Of course. We can go to the library. I'm baking bread with my mother this morning, but when I'm done, we can go. I'll have to come up with a reason why I need to go to town. Papa could take us." Annie tried thinking of possible excuses. They could walk, but it would cut into their time. "I can say I'm working on a special project."

"That sounds believable," Sam said smiling. "I'll wait in your room while you're baking."

Annie watched Sam disappear then she went into the kitchen and grabbed her apron. "Are we baking white bread or wheat?"

"I thought we'd do cornbread. It's easier and doesn't take so long." Mrs. Harper put a bowl on the counter.

"I love cornbread." Annie was thankful that they were baking something that was quick. That would give her more time at the library with Sam. Now she had to figure out how she was going to get there.

"Mama? Do you think Papa could take me to the library today? I want to work on a special project." Annie thought asking her mother first might give her a clue about whether this idea would work.

"School is out for the summer. What kind of project?" Mama asked.

"There's something I want to know more about. You know how much I enjoy learning. Please Mama? Do you think you could ask Papa for me? I don't know if he's still upset with me." Annie put on her best-begging face.

"It's all right with me but you will still have to ask your father. He was going into town today anyway, to help the Pastor fix a window." Eileen stirred the batter.

Annie saw that her mother was almost finished mixing the cornbread. "Do you want me to pour the batter into the pan?"

"Why don't you go ask your Papa if he'll take you? I'll finish up here." Mrs. Harper smiled at her daughter.

"Thank you, Mama. You're the best." Annie ran outside to find her father and was delighted that he agreed to take her to the library. She noticed that Sam was right beside her, his huge smile shining across his face.

CHAPTER EIGHT

Annie arranged herself in the wagon, leaning into the bags of grain and pulling her cloak tighter. It was a chilly day, but the sky was clear and sunny. Sam sat across from her, his head turning to notice everything that was going on around him. Annie decided to leave Sadie at home. Joseph was almost finished harnessing Rosie.

"I'm glad Papa is taking us to the library," Annie whispered to Sam.

Sam leaned back, his hands behind his head. "Yes indeed. So this is how you go places?"

"Yes Sam. We can't instantly go places, like you." Annie giggled, wondering what it would feel like to go somewhere by merely thinking about it.

"What's this project you're doing?" Joseph asked his daughter, as he climbed up onto the bench.

Not prepared for the question, Annie struggled to find something that would sound reasonable. "Uh, I'm doing research on mythology. I was reading a book about Pegasus, you know that flying horse that the Greeks talked about? There is a lot of information at the library about mythology." Annie hated lying but in a way, it was true. Annie did enjoy learning about mythology. "...and then I want to draw pictures of what I learn so I can hang them on my wall."

"That does sound interesting. I'd love to see your drawings when you're finished." Joseph snapped the reins. "Let's go, Rosie." The wagon lurched forward as the big mare pulled on the harness.

Annie hoped that her father didn't ask any other questions about her project. "Papa, how old is Rosie now?" Annie asked, hoping to change the subject.

"She's about fifteen, four years older than you." Joseph kept his gaze on the road.

"Maybe some time you'll let me hold the reins." Annie wanted to create a diversion.

"How about now? Hop up here next to me," Mr. Harper shouted.

Annie crawled up to the bench and scooted close to her father. "So, what do I do first?"

"Here, hold these reins in your right hand and these in your left. Keep them laced through your fingers. You don't want them falling out of your hands." Mr. Harper handed the reins to Annie.

"Like this?" Annie felt the pull of the strong horse. It was harder than she imagined.

"Perfect. Now if you want to turn, you move the reins to that side. Rosie can feel them on her neck." Joseph helped Annie steer a little to the right, then to the left. "And when you want to stop, you pull straight back and say 'whoa'."

Annie pulled back on the reins and shouted, "Whoa, Rosie." Annie saw the horse's ears tilt back and the horse stopped. "I did it. Papa, I did it."

"Yes, you did. Good job. Now let me take over. There are some holes in the road coming up. But you can stay up here with me if you'd like." Joseph smiled at his daughter.

Annie thought about Sam who was sitting in the back. "This bench is way too bouncy."

"Okay. It's more comfortable on those sacks of grain. This bench is pretty hard." Joseph held onto Annie's arm as she hopped into the back.

"I wonder what we're going to find out at the library?" Sam yelled above the noise.

Annie spoke directly into Sam's ear. "I don't know but at least I can turn the pages for you and the librarian can show us where to look."

"There's a room where they keep all the old survey books. I heard someone talking about old records that are stored there," Sam replied.

They finally pulled up in front of the library. Annie was happy the ride was over.

"While you are in the library, I'm going to the church. I'm helping the pastor fix a broken window. He wanted it done by this Sunday since it's Easter. Walk over to the church when you're done at the library." Mr. Harper helped Annie out of the wagon.

"I was thinking that I'll walk home. I don't know how long I'm going to be." Annie wanted to make sure she and Sam didn't have to rush. "I saw some flowers in a meadow the other day. I'll go there and pick some for Mama. It shouldn't take me long to get home. I know all the shortcuts." Annie didn't like walking home but she would have Sam with her. As long as they left by three, they could get home before supper.

"Sure. You've walked home before, although I wish you had brought Sadie," Papa replied.

"I can't take her in the library. That's why I didn't bring her. I'll be okay, Papa. I walk home from school sometimes. It doesn't take that long." Annie hoped her father would give his permission.

"Do you promise you'll be careful? Your mother is the one who will worry most, you know." Mr. Harper hesitated.

"Yes Papa. I promise. Bet I get home before you do." Annie knew her father would finish before she and Sam were done.

"Alright. See you at supper." Mr. Harper snapped the reins and steered Rosie down the road.

Annie waited until her father was out of sight. She and Sam hopped up the steps to the big, white stone library.

"Hello Annie. What a pleasure to see you. Most of the children don't come here during the summer." The librarian welcomed the young girl as she walked by the large wooden counter.

"It's nice to see you, Mrs. Gordon. I need to find some information for a friend," said Annie, not knowing what to ask.

"What type of information?" the librarian asked.

"I am looking for books about this area - things that happened the past hundred years," replied Annie, using her most polite voice.

"That's very specific. Why would you need that?" the librarian quizzed.

"Uh, my friend wanted to find information about his family. He's visiting but his grandparents were from around here. He's doing gynology," Annie stated. "He gave me some names and dates to look up. He had wanted to come with me but he had chores to do."

"You mean genealogy?" Mrs. Gordon laughed. "I hope your friend can research for himself. It is very interesting."

"He trusts me. I'm going to take him whatever I find." Annie surprised herself that she almost remembered the right word.

"What an interesting project. I know exactly where to find what you're looking for. Please, follow me." Mrs. Gordon walked down a dark narrow hall, past the rows of books and racks of magazines. "This room doesn't get used much, but it's where the archives are stored."

"The archives?" Annie asked.

"Let me show you." Mrs. Gordon led her to a door, way in the back of the library. "It might be a bit dusty." The woman opened the door and turned on the light. "All the records of Cornwall are kept in here. They are arranged by date. Be careful and use the step stool. We don't need you falling, now do we? There's a little table over there where you can take notes. These books must remain here so you will have to write down the information. You did bring paper, didn't you?"

"Of course. Thank you, Mrs. Gordon," Annie replied.

"I must go back to my counter. Please let me know when you're done so I can turn out the lights." The librarian left the room.

"Finally. I thought she'd never leave," Sam responded.

"At least she was helpful. Let's get started." Annie was eager to start pulling books from the shelves.

"I was born on September 22, 1805. I want to locate information about when I died, and also about my mother. Maybe that will give me some clues. What if the way I died had something to do with why I didn't go to heaven?" Sam asked. "Maybe I did something bad."

Annie wandered through the aisles reading out the titles on the book spines. "Census surveys. Looks like there's some information in these. They are labeled by year." The young girl pulled down one of the leather-covered books. "This one has 1800 written on it."

Sam leaned over Annie's shoulder and watched as the girl turned the pages. "Look for Samuel Charles Sullivan. That's my full name."

"The names are listed by town. Here's Penzance. There are four Sullivans. Andrew, Brian, Robert, and Charles. There are no women's names." Annie kept reading. "Maybe these are landowners."

"There must be one for births and deaths," Sam commented.

Annie pulled down an old green leather-covered journal. "This one's dated 1804. Here are more. All are in Penzance. Andrew, Brian, Robert, Charles, and Martha. Is your mother's name Martha?"

"Yes, that's her name. I wonder if she was married to one of those men. Maybe my father is Charles. After all, my middle name is Charles." Sam wanted so much to believe that these could be his parents.

Annie jotted down the names Charles and Martha, and also the year. The hours went by much too fast. "We've been here a long time and we aren't finding anything. We better go." Annie was disappointed. "We need to look somewhere else."

Sam nodded, his face sad. "Thank you for trying."

Annie put all the books back and gathered up her notes. Annie and Sam walked back through the hall and approached the counter. "Thank you, Mrs. Gordon. I'm finished now."

"Did you find what you were looking for?" the librarian asked. "Yes, I took lots of notes." Annie waved as she walked towards the exit.

"Splendid. I love it when young people do research. There is so much history to be learned." Mrs. Gordon's face lit up.

The two children walked down the wide white steps of the library and turned left towards the church. The spire was visible from anywhere in Willow Glen, so it was easy to find.

"There's Rosie. Papa's still here." Annie climbed into the wagon and saw that Sam was already sitting on a bag of grain. "You sure move fast."

"There are some advantages to being a ghost," Sam chuckled.

I wonder how much longer Papa will be. I better go tell him I'm here since he thinks I'm walking home." She looked at Sam who appeared disappointed. "Sam, sorry we couldn't find anything at the library."

"That's okay. It's not meant to be. I guess I'm not supposed to go to heaven," he commented.

"Don't say that. You are going to get to heaven, I promise you," Annie said. "Please don't give up." Annie reached over to touch Sam's hand, but her hand went right through him. Tears welled up in her eyes as she thought of how lonely Sam must have felt all these years.

"Have you seen the garden? That should cheer you up." Annie climbed down and walked towards the garden. Sam was right behind.

"Roses. I love roses." Sam's smile grew large.

"Me too. We named our horse Rosie because she likes to eat the petals." Annie watched Sam smile again as he floated through the maze of bushes. A white picket fence surrounded the garden. A cobblestone path led from the road to the front door. A large wooden door served as the entrance into the quaint country church.

Sam leaned down to smell a rose. "I wish I could still smell."

"Pastor Clark planted these. He's a wonderful gardener." Annie picked a rose and placed it in her pocket.

"You know, Sam? I was thinking. Remember at the library when you mentioned looking for a book about births and deaths?" Annie asked.

"Yes. There must be records like that somewhere," Sam replied.

"What about a church?" Annie's eyes lit up.

"Do you think?" Sam's eyes grew big.

"I know where the storage room is." Annie hurried to a side door and opened it. "It's this way."

Annie pulled open the heavy wooden side door and saw her father on a ladder working on the window. The Pastor was holding the ladder. Their voices muffled, Annie couldn't make out what they were saying. Annie whispered to Sam. "The room is this way. Follow me."

The children walked through a back hallway and opened the door to a small room. Cleaning supplies, books, and assorted tools filled the room. "Over here. Maybe they keep records in this trunk." Annie lifted the heavy lid. There were wide leather straps that attached the lid to the base. Annie leaned into the deep trunk, Sam right next to her. Suddenly, both Annie and Sam fell head first into the large trunk and the lid slammed down above them.

"Push. Push harder," Sam yelled at Annie.

"It won't budge. I can't get it open," Annie shouted back.

"Help. Help," Annie yelled. She hoped her father could hear her, yet realized he probably thought she was still at the library.

"Wait. What's happening," shouted Sam with alarm.

There was a loud whooshing sound. "Sam, do you hear that?" Annie said.

"Yes. It sounds like a windstorm," Sam replied.

"Now it feels like we're moving. Something's lifting us up." The trunk began tilting and rocking. Annie bounced back and forth, bumping into the sides of the large trunk. "Sam, I'm scared. What's happening?"

"We're falling," Sam shouted.

The box twirled, tipped, and tumbled, the children tossing back and forth. It landed with a heavy thud. Everything was still. Annie felt her head and noticed a big bump forming. She then felt an arm next to her. "Sam, is that you?"

"Of course it's me. Annie, you're holding onto my arm. I can feel you!" Sam exclaimed.

"How can that be?" Annie couldn't see inside the trunk. Everything was dark. She felt her hand holding onto an arm. Annie slowly lifted the lid of the trunk, enough to barely peek outside. "Sam, you're not going to believe this."

"Believe what?" Sam helped Annie push the lid open.

Annie's eyes grew big as she saw her friend helping her. "You pushed the trunk lid open. Sam, how are you doing that?" Sam was holding up the heavy lid.

"I can feel it and I feel you touching me. Annie, I can feel," Sam shouted.

The two climbed out of the trunk and saw that they were in a very thick forest. "Where's the church? Where are we?" Annie's fear grew.

The trees were tall and the forest seemed very thick. There were berry bushes everywhere. Annie could see that the bushes were moving. "Sam, those bushes look like they're coming towards us." Annie looked for an escape.

"I see a trail over there." Sam pointed.

"Run!" Annie and the boy ran towards the trail, the bushes now moving faster towards them. "How can bushes move like that?" Annie's voice trembled in fear.

"I don't know but I think you better run faster," Sam shouted.

"Over here. Run this way," said a deep, gruff voice.

"It's coming from over there," Annie yelled. They ran towards the voice.

"Quickly, get inside," bellowed a stern voice from inside a little house.

The children ran towards the cottage, the bushes nipping at their heels. "Hurry Sam." Annie reached for Sam's hand. They hurled themselves through the open doorway, rolling past the threshold as the door shut behind them. A little shaken, the children picked themselves up from the floor.

Annie looked around and saw a cozy little room with a warm crackling fire burning in the fireplace.

"That was close. You almost got brambled," said the raspy voice.

Annie turned around and looked up. Standing before her was a creature, unlike anything she had ever seen. He was close to her own height but much wider. Two white horns were sticking out of each side of his head and his large, bulbous nose was speckled with spots. He had ragged looking gray hair and enormous feet with tufts of hair on each toe. His flesh tone skin had a pink glow. Two long teeth protruded out of each side of his mouth. The creature was hairy from head to toe, except for his face and hands. He wore only a shirt since his bottom half was thick with grayish-brown fur, much like a bear.

Annie jumped back, frightened. "Who are you?" her voice shaking in fear.

"Please don't be afraid. I am Ornoth, the troll of this forest." The strange creature walked towards Sam. "Looks like you are hurt. Let me tend to that."

"Hurt? What do you mean hurt?" Sam asked.

"You have a big cut on your forehead. You're bleeding." Ornoth held out a cloth to the young boy.

Sam noticed the blood. "But I'm dead. How can I be bleeding?" He dabbed at the cut on his head.

Ornoth looked confused. "Dead? Why would you say that? You look very alive to me."

"You 'are' bleeding, Sam," Annie replied. She walked over to her friend and reached for his hand. "I can feel you. You're as solid as I am." Annie wondered how she could feel her ghost friend.

"How can this be?" Sam fainted and slumped to the ground.

Annie watched as Ornoth picked up the young boy and placed him on a straw-filled bed.

"That's a large gash on his head. I have the perfect thing." The troll disappeared into another room and came back with some bottles. "This tincture will help."

Annie watched Ornoth pour something from a bottle onto Sam's wound. The troll then wrapped the boy's head in strips of cloth. Ornoth placed a few drops from another bottle into Sam's mouth.

"He needs to rest now. Looks like you two have been through a trying time." The troll pulled a blanket over the boy. He then turned his attention to Annie. "He will sleep for a while. I gave him a sleeping potion."

"A sleeping potion? Are you a sorcerer?" Annie was scared now and backed up away from the shaggy creature. What if this was all a dream? She tried waking up but still felt the same.

"No, I am not a sorcerer, however, I do know about potions. Don't they have trolls where you come from?" Ornoth seemed confused.

"No. We do not have trolls. There is no such thing," Annie commented. This is getting crazy, she thought. Why can't I wake up?

"Obviously there is such a thing because I'm standing right here, right in front of you." Ornoth placed his hands on his hips.

Annie felt inside her pocket and felt the rose she had picked at the church. "This wasn't a dream," she thought.

"I can assure you, young lady, that you are very much awake. Please, sit down and tell me how you found yourself here." Ornoth led Annie to a small table and chairs in the kitchen.

Annie decided she needed to trust the troll. After all, he was helping them. He didn't seem dangerous. "We were in Willow Glen, at the church."

"Willow Glen. Where is that?" Ornoth questioned.

"It's the town where I live. We were at the church and we leaned over the trunk but fell completely inside. Then it began moving and twisted and turned. We landed here," said Annie as she described what had happened.

Ornoth scratched his head. "That's an amazing trunk if it brought you here."

"And then, when we crawled out of the trunk, the bushes chased us. We didn't know where to go or what to do." Annie's fear rose again as she retold the story.

"I can explain the bushes." Ornoth got up and went to the window. "The bushes have pulled back. You are safe right now." The scraggly troll set a cup of tea in front of Annie, and another for himself. "Please, have some moss tea. It will make you feel better. We will talk more later."

59

Annie peered into the cup seeing green water with a bit of moss swirling around. She took a sip and was surprised how sweet it was. She took another sip and felt herself getting sleepy. The room faded away and all became black.

CHAPTER NINE

"Annie. Wake up." Sam shook his sleeping friend.

"Wha…what?" Annie opened her eyes. "Where am I?"

"You've been sleeping. It's morning. We must've slept all night." Sam helped Annie sit up. "Ornoth fixed breakfast for us. He is waiting in the kitchen. Come on. Get up. I'm hungry." He still was amazed at the human feelings and sensations he now had. "There are biscuits and berries and cheese. I can't wait to taste food again. Hurry up."

Annie stood up and looked around the room. "You mean this isn't a dream?"

"No. It's real. I'm alive again. I have a bit of a headache but Ornoth told me he has a tincture that will make it not hurt so much." Sam was overjoyed. He wanted to explain to Annie how it felt, but there were no words that could describe his feelings.

"Alright but first I need to find the loo. Ornoth, where can I go to, uh, you know, freshen up?" Annie looked around the cottage.

At first, Ornoth seemed confused. "Ahhh. You need to go to the tree."

"The tree? No. I don't need a tree, I need…" Annie crossed her legs.

"Annie, there's a privy. It's behind the cottage." Sam led Annie to a back door and pointed at the small wooden structure not too far from the house. He had already used it with no problem. Considering it had been over a hundred years since he needed one, he was surprised how much came natural. "Guess having tea last night did something to my body. Had to go as soon as I woke up."

Annie laughed. "I bet that felt odd to you."

"Here. Take this with you." Ornoth handed Annie a stick.

"What's this for?" Annie asked.

"It's charmed to keep the brambles away, but only for a few minutes. You don't want those bushes to start chasing you again, do you?" Ornoth warned.

"What if I need longer than a few minutes?" Annie asked.

"Not sure. It never takes me longer than a that." Ornoth pulled at the whiskers on his pointed chin.

"I'll stand guard, Annie. Be quick. I want to eat. My mouth has been watering ever since I woke up." Sam's stomach growled. He waited by the door and watched to make sure Annie made it to the privy. He saw that she had a firm grip on the stick and was wasting no time.

She quickly found her way back to the cottage. "There. Satisfied?" She snapped at Ornoth and Sam. "There were spiders out there. I don't think I like this arrangement."

Ornoth looked confused. "Sorry. I'm not sure what young ladies want."

Sam didn't care what his friend thought. He was anxious to dig into the bowls and plates of food he had been watching Ornoth prepare. "Time to eat." Sam pulled a chair from the table and plopped down.

"I have to wash up first. Is there a sink? I need soap." Annie looked down at her hands.

Sam glared at Annie. "If you don't hurry, I'm eating without you." He had already piled his plate with an assortment of food.
"Over there." Ornoth pointed at a basin in the corner next to a jug of water and a mirror.

"Thank you." Annie did not seem amused. "I was beginning to think you were uncivilized."

Ornoth again looked confused. "Uh, uncivilized? Not sure what you mean."

"I'm not waiting for you." Sam grabbed a biscuit and shoved it into his mouth. "This is delicious." He grabbed another one and covered it with jam and pushed it into his mouth. "So good," he remarked in a muffled voice.

"Slow down there, young man. There's no need to rush," remarked Ornoth, with a laugh. He moved a chair next to the boy. "But you don't understand. I haven't eaten in over a hundred years." Sam stuffed more food into his mouth.

Annie finally sat down, her hands smelling of soap and her hair tidied up. "You don't have to eat like a pig, Sam. At least you can have some manners."

"I'm sorry. I should've waited for you," said Sam, trying to sound apologetic. Annie was annoying him. Why did she have to be so prissy?

"We are guests in Ornoth's house." Annie arranged her pinafore. "Have manners, Sam." Annie frowned at Sam as he wiped his mouth with his sleeve.

Ornoth looked puzzled but went back to his bowl of moss porridge. "You children sure are unusual. Fergus should be back soon. He will know much more about your situation."

"Fergus? Who is Fergus?" Sam looked up from his plate, jam dripping down his chin.

"Fergus is my good friend. He lives here with me." Ornoth picked up his bowl and slurped down the mossy broth until the bowl was empty. He let out a large belch.

Annie looked up, her face showing a look of disgust. "Mama sure wouldn't like that."

"Like what?" Ornoth asked.

"You belched. We don't do that at the table," Annie remarked.

"So where do you do it then?" Ornoth asked, green moss still dangling from his teeth.

Sam laughed so hard, his belly shook. "I think what Annie is trying to say is that where she lives, they have manners. They wash up before eating. They have an inside loo. They are sophisticated." Sam knew Annie was upset. But here they were in some strange forest, in a troll's cabin, drinking tea made from moss, and worrying about man-eating bushes. Who cares about manners at a time like this?

Annie kicked Sam. "You were nicer as a dead boy. I'm going home." Annie got out of her chair and headed for the door. "I only wanted to help you and now you make fun of me." Annie's eyes filled with tears.

"Wait. You can't go out there." Ornoth jumped up to stop the girl. "The Black Thatcher is out there. It is too dangerous."

"I don't care who's out there. I'm going home," shouted Annie as her sobs got louder.

"Wait, wait. I can't let you leave. It's not safe. I sure wish Fergus was here." Ornoth grabbed at the girl's dress but it was too late. The door had already swung open and Annie had stepped out onto the porch.

She did not get far when a large crow, about the same size as Annie, hopped in front of her, pushing her back inside. "Who might we have here?" The huge black bird cackled.

Annie screamed, then fell back, falling into Ornoth's arms. Sam jumped up from the table and ran towards his friend. "You're scaring her. Stop," Sam shouted. Even though he had teased his friend, he still wanted to protect her.

"Fergus. I am so glad you're finally here," Ornoth said with relief. "We have guests. This is Sam and Annie. They are visiting from Willow Glen."

Fergus waddled into the cottage and shut the door behind him, his feathers ruffled from the wind. "Hmmm. Human children. We don't see them in the forest often. I don't think we've ever had children visit, have we?" Fergus's voice sounded scholarly and dignified.

"I was hoping you might be able to help them, Fergus. They have an interesting story to tell. I think we're finished eating, at least Sam and I are finished. Annie doesn't seem to be very hungry." Ornoth led the group to the hearth room.

"First things first." Fergus hopped into the kitchen and poured himself some moss tea. He had no trouble holding the mug with his large wing. The human-sized bird then made himself comfortable in one of the large chairs near the fireplace.

Ornoth motioned to the children to sit on the hearth. "These young people seem to have come from another time. Sam says he had been dead and now is very much alive."

"That is a curious story." Fergus waved a wing towards the children. "Is this all true?"

Sam hadn't said anything since the large bird arrived at the cottage. What does one say to a human-sized talking crow? "I don't think I've ever met a bird that talks, although I did read something about parrots. They can talk."

"Parrots? Ah yes. Tropical birds. None of those around here." Fergus sipped his tea. "But again, is it true, what Ornoth said?"

Sam observed the large bird and then looked across the table at the troll. This was too much. Trolls, talking crows, cursed bushes. What more could happen? The forest where they landed appeared enchanted or bewitched.

"Uh, yes, it is true. But seeing you, a talking crow as tall as we are, is a bit hard to believe. Why should we talk to you? How do we know that you aren't a figment of our imagination?"

Ornoth grumbled. "That was rude, young man. Fergus is my friend."

Fergus held up his wing to Ornoth. Let me answer. "Good question." Fergus leaned over and pecked Sam in the arm.

"Ouch. What did you do that for?" Sam rubbed his arm.

"I would imagine that if I were a figment of your imagination, you wouldn't have felt that, and you wouldn't have a red welt forming on your skin," Fergus remarked.

Sam looked down at his arm and saw a spot swelling. "You didn't have to peck me," he moaned. "Then yes, I guess you're real but this sure isn't normal."

"And you, time traveling and coming back from the dead? You think that sounds normal? And as for why you should be talking to me. Because I know everything that goes on in this forest. Nothing escapes me because I can go places most can't. I can fly above the forest. I don't need to go through the bushes. The Black Thatcher can't bramble me because he can't catch me," Fergus stated proudly.

"We don't even know what this Black Thatcher is. And we don't know what being brambled is, either. We do know that we want to go home," said Sam, his voice quivering with fear. Sam stood up and pulled Annie to her feet. "Let's go, Annie. They can't keep us here. We need to find the trunk. Maybe it can take us back."

"Wait. If you go out there, you will never get back to your home. Believe me. The Black Thatcher is waiting for you," announced Fergus, his tone serious.

"I don't believe you," said Sam defiantly.
"Then see for yourself. Take a step outside and see what happens," said Fergus, daring the young boy.

"Fine. I will." Sam opened the door and walked towards the white picket fence. He looked back towards Annie. "Come with me. If we run fast, we should be fine."

Annie hesitated at the door. "Sam, the bushes are moving. I think you should come back inside."

"You believe their rubbish?" Sam chuckled. "Look. There's noth…" Suddenly a vine wrapped itself around Sam's ankle. Sam fell, his body being pulled out of the yard and into the forest. "Help!" Sam screamed. The vine pulled harder and faster. Sam's head hit the stone path. He knew he'd made a mistake. What should he do now?

Large black wings swooped down over the boy's struggling form, the crow's beak pecking and pounding on the thick thorny vine. "Grab my wing," Fergus shouted to Sam.

Sam grasped a handful of feathers and let Fergus battle the twisting, thrashing vine. The vine snapped and Fergus turned and took three large hops towards the door. Ornoth pulled Sam and Fergus inside, slamming the door behind them.

Annie ran to her friend and wrapped her arms around him. "Sam, are you alright?"

"I, I, did… didn't, be… believe th… them." The boy's voice shook in between his sobs. "Fergus saved me." Sam felt the bump forming on his head. He was ashamed. He should've listened.

"Yes, he did," Ornoth announced sternly. "You are a foolish boy and almost got yourself brambled."

"What would've happened?" Sam asked. "What is brambled?"

"The Black Thatcher would've added you to the brambles, the berry bushes," Fergus remarked as he struggled to catch his breath. "He detects life energy of animals, fairies, elves, pixies, even trolls. I imagine a human life force would be even stronger. He then bewitches them and turns them into berries in the bramble bushes. Those are what you see moving. Every berry has someone, or something trapped inside. He has an army of creatures who serve him. Upon his command, they pick the berries and turn them into juice. When his own life force weakens, he drinks the juice. The energy from those brambled becomes his, and he is able to live forever, or until the berries run out." Fergus's wings spread as he narrated the story. "You would've been inside a berry; I guarantee you that."

Sam's sobs became louder. "I want to go home. I would rather be a ghost like I was before, than be trapped here." He thought it would be wonderful to be alive, but having to feel fear again, was almost more than he could handle.

"We have to let them help us, Sam," said Annie, her concern clear. "Ornoth saved us and now Fergus saved you. What more proof do you need?"

"But I thought you wanted to go home?" He gazed at Annie, hoping she could reassure him. He was supposed to be the strong one but it seemed that Annie was always consoling him.

"I do want to go home but as you have seen, there is no way we can get back to the trunk. And even if we did, how do we know it would even take us home? We need to listen to Ornoth and Fergus. They know this forest better than we do," announced Annie.

Sam wiped the tears from his eyes. "I'm sorry. It's been a long time since I was afraid. When you're dead, there isn't much that scares you."

"I think we have work to do. You want to get back home, right?" Ornoth asked.

"Yes," the children replied in unison.

The troll continued. "And you want to know why you ended up here, correct?"

"Yes."

"Fergus, what do you know about Willow Glen and why might these young people have ended up here?" Ornoth turned to his friend.

Scratching his head with one wing, Fergus pondered. "There have been humans in this forest before but if my recollections are accurate, only one claimed to have been from another time. It was many, many years ago. I never met her. I have heard rumors, though. This was before the Black Thatcher arrived."

Ornoth struggled to remember. "My memories aren't as sharp as yours, my friend. What happened to this woman?"

"I don't know. She was there one minute then, she vanished the next. I thought the fairies took her. You know, like when they take the dead to the land in between blinks." Fergus described what he could.

"Oh yes. In between blinks. She's here until she's there," Ornoth replied. "Do you know who this woman might be and how did she die?"

"I don't know but I think I know who might be able to tell us." Fergus was deep in thought.

"Children. I have an idea. I think I know a way to get you away from the Black Thatcher," said Fergus.

"What's your idea?" Sam asked with excitement.

"Ornoth has a map of the forest. There are some hidden caves that the pixies told us about, but only because they are our close friends. We try to look out for each other when we can." Fergus hopped towards the desk. "I think it's in here." Fergus opened a drawer. "Yes, here it is." The crow pulled up a rolled-up paper tied with twine.

"Lay it out here on the table." Ornoth cleared a space. The parchment was old and brown around the edges. Sketches of green trees, brown paths, and gray boulders filled the page. Ornoth's gnarled, pointed finger traced the path from the cottage to a clump of bushes. "I think it's here, beneath this clump of shrubs."

"Yes. That's the one I was thinking of." Fergus's feathers fluffed up. "It's not too far. I believe we can get you there safely, but we'll have to have a plan. The Black Thatcher will be waiting. We need to trick him."

"But how?" Annie sounded concerned.

"We will create a diversion," the bird stated.

"Fergus, I can go out the front door and get the Black Thatcher's attention. I will stall him while you take the children to the cave. They can sit on your back and you could fly them there." Ornoth's plan seemed possible.

"I am not sure I can carry both children, but I might be able to carry one at a time." Fergus tilted his head, his black eyes reflecting the children's faces.

"But how will you prevent the Black Thatcher from coming after you, Ornoth?" Annie reached for the troll's hand. "I would hate if anything horrid happened to you."

"Not to worry. I am old and my life force is probably weak. Maybe he won't notice me as quickly." Ornoth tried to alleviate the young girl's fears.

"Then it's settled. I have some supplies to get ready for you and then we will be on our way." Fergus hopped into the back room and returned with two knapsacks. "You will need water and food. Also torches." Fergus filled the sacks. "And you must promise to stay together. When you get into the caves, it will be very dark. The torches will light your way, but the shadows can trick you. Here is a rope to tie yourself together. Do you promise?"

"Yes, we promise," Sam and Annie replied together.

"And another thing. Here." Ornoth placed a vial in each of the children's hands. "Keep these hidden in your pockets. You will know when to use them. Do not tell anyone you have them."

"What do they do?" Sam asked, placing his vial in his pocket.

"You will know when the time is right. More information at this time is not necessary." Ornoth ruffled Sam's hair. "I guess this is good-bye." Ornoth huddled with the children. "It has been my pleasure to meet you. I hope you have a safe journey and maybe one day, you will visit again."

Sam knew that the crow and troll wanted to help, but the thought of flying through the air on the back of an oversize bird was a bit scary. Sam looked at Annie and wondered what she must be thinking. Did she expect him to take care of her? What if he was more afraid than she was?

A tear ran down Annie's face. "You are such a kind troll. I will never be afraid of trolls again. I am sorry I was rude to you." She hugged Ornoth.

"Thank you for all you have done for us. I don't know how we can repay you?" Sam held out his hand.

"Be safe." Ornoth shook Sam's hand, then pulled him close and offered a hug. "Make sure you follow Fergus's directions. There is still danger in this plan but if anyone can make it work, Fergus can."

The children nodded, put on their knapsacks and tightened the buckles. Sam wondered if he should grab some extra food but decided he had eaten plenty. His body might not know how to handle that much food. Besides, Fergus probably preferred them to be as light as possible.

"Ornoth, I will take Annie first and then come back for Sam. Don't go outside until you hear my signal, two caws, and a whistle." Fergus gave final instructions to his friend.

"Two caws and a whistle. I will be listening." Ornoth stationed himself at the front door.

"Annie, climb on board and hold on tight. I tend to swerve." Fergus bent down and allowed the young girl to grab hold. Hopping out the backdoor, Fergus took three leaps and bounded into the air.

Sam watched as Annie soared into the sky, her braids blowing behind her, her body perched on a large, black crow. He crossed his fingers. The time seemed to crawl, as Sam and Ornoth listened for the signal. There was nothing. Ten minutes. Twenty minutes, and then finally, Fergus tumbled into the cottage.

"Made it. Hit a bit of turbulence but Annie is safe and sound waiting inside the cave. But we must hurry. I saw the brambles moving towards the house. The Black Thatcher suspects something. The signal would've tipped him off. Ornoth, I think you will need to distract him. I don't want him heading for the cave," Fergus replied while catching his breath. "Sam, hop on. Your turn."

Sam climbed onto the crow's back, waving at Ornoth one last time. He grabbed a handful of feathers and hoped he could hold on. Fergus soared into the air, high above the forest. Sam felt the air hitting his face and stinging his eyes. It was hard to keep his eyes open; they watered so much. Below, he could see the tops of the trees and the roof of the cottage. Sam looked back and saw the bushes moving towards the cottage. He saw Ornoth standing on the path and then saw Ornoth tumble to the ground.

"Fergus. We must go back. Ornoth fell and the bushes are moving towards him," shouted Sam as loud as he could, but Fergus kept flying. "We have to go back. Ornoth is in trouble." Still, the crow continued, the cottage getting further and further behind.

The ground loomed closer and Fergus swooped down, sliding into the damp soil. "The cave is behind those bushes. Annie is waiting there. Make sure you light your torch and tie yourselves together," instructed Fergus.

Now that Fergus could hear him, Sam shouted, "Ornoth is in trouble. The brambles got him. I saw him fall and I tried to tell you, but you couldn't hear me. Please go help him."

Fergus took a running start and swooped into the air, tipping his wing to say good-bye. "Stay safe." The crow's voice faded in the wind.

§ § §

The vines curled tighter and tighter around Ornoth's leg. He struggled to pull them off but to no avail. He saw the brambles moving closer and closer as the thorny appendages kept a grip on his old body. It was getting harder and harder to breathe as the vines worked their way up around his chest. The more he struggled, the tighter the vines gripped. He gasped and sputtered, barely able to breathe. "Good-bye Fergus. I hope you got the children to the cave." Ornoth's last thoughts were of his best friend and the children. Everything turned black.

Wings flayed and his sharp beak tore and ripped, as Fergus pulled the vines from his friend. "Hold on, Ornoth. Hold on," Fergus shouted. Black feathers filled the air as Fergus struggled. With one last tug, the vines came loose.

Ornoth's lungs filled with air as he choked and gulped. He reached for his throat. "Air. I need air," the troll gasped. He looked up and saw the large shiny bird huddled in a heap next to him. "Fergus. Fergus. Are you alright?"

There was no reply. Ornoth pulled himself to his feet and went to the crumpled crow. "Fergus, can you hear me?"

Fergus moved and slowly lifted his head. Seeing Ornoth, he said, "We must get inside. Hurry." The two stumbled to the door, holding on to each other.

The door slammed with a bang behind them. "I thought I was dead. Everything turned black." Ornoth still struggled for breath.

Fergus also gasped. "Those were my black feathers, silly old troll." He pointed at the path, which was now lined with black silky feathers. "They'll grow back." The crow and troll laughed with nervous relief and then held each other tight.

Fergus helped Ornoth to the sofa. "Let me get us some moss tea. I know that will calm our shattered nerves."

"Are the children alright? Did you find the cave?" Ornoth accepted the tea that Fergus had prepared.

"Yes, although I wasn't able to say proper good-byes. There wasn't enough time," said Fergus, looking disappointed.

"I'm sure they knew how you felt. They are now in the land of the pixies. We can only hope that they will find answers there." Ornoth settled back on the sofa, the soothing moss tea putting him into a soft slumber. "Thank you, you silly old bird. I don't know what I would do without you." Ornoth reached for the crow, stroking his back which was now missing large areas of feathers.

"For you, anything my friend." Fergus snuggled next to the exhausted creature. Soon they both were softly snoring in the cozy cottage.

CHAPTER TEN

Annie held out her torch for Sam to light it. He had already lit his. They were already inside the pixie cave but until the torches, it was too dark to see. Annie realized that it looked very familiar.

"I think we can speak normal now. I doubt the Black Thatcher can come in here. Looks like we can go a few different ways. There are tunnels leading right, middle and left." Sam scanned the space. "The path looks pretty solid and the tunnels are large enough we can stand up. At least we won't have to crawl."

Annie brushed off the dirt from her clothes. "I'm going to follow you." She didn't want to tell Sam about the pixie cave she had found near Willow Glen. She had promised and she intended to keep that promise, even now.

Sam stopped to tie himself to Annie. "I almost forgot. Fergus said we need to be tied together."

"Don't walk too fast." Annie tugged on the rope to make sure the knot held.

"I will go slow. I want to make sure there aren't any holes or cliffs or anything." Sam waved the torch back and forth. "The path seems pretty dry. Odd that the walls are wet."

Annie touched the tunnel wall. "Sam, they're not wet."

Sam also touched the wall. "So why are they so shiny?"

"It's crystals." Annie held her torch closer to the walls. "Look, the walls are lined with purple crystals. Sam, they're the same type of crystal I have in my pocket, like the one I found in the forest when I found you, remember?" She could at least tell him that much.

"How could I forget? That's the only reason you could see me." Sam remembered their first meeting.

"Do you think…" Sam asked.

"...that it came from this cave?" Annie finished the question.

"Yah. Even though the forest here doesn't look anything like our forest in Willow Glen, maybe there are caves there, too. I'm glad this isn't water running down the walls. We would be sloshing through puddles." Sam kept moving forward, checking for holes.

The tunnel curved and twisted. Every so often there would be a larger space, almost like a room, but no one came to their rescue. "I'm beginning to think Fergus and Ornoth are playing a trick on us. I haven't heard or seen a pixie." Sam's frustration was building.

Annie thought about her secret. Maybe this was not the time to be worrying about promises. "Sam, I need you to promise me something," said Annie, her face serious. "I didn't tell you everything about my crystal. I made a promise."

"Promise to who?" Sam inquired.

"I can't tell you yet, but I need you to trust me," stated Annie. If this rescue didn't work, she didn't need to tell him anything else.

"But what's the promise?" Sam was still confused.

"I can't tell you yet. Please promise that you will keep my secret," said Annie with a serious tone.

"I guess but do I have any other choice? How can I promise to keep a secret I don't even know?" Sam remarked.

"Let me get in front of you." Annie squeezed through the tight passageway, careful not to burn Sam with her torch. "I have a plan." Annie led them through the tunnel until they reached a large pool of water. Yes, she remembered this. It was Shimmer. This had to be the place. Annie pulled out her crystal. "Phillip. This is Annie. I need you."

"Who is Phillip?" Sam asked.

"Shhhhh. Be quiet," Annie snapped at Sam. "Phillip. This is Annie. Are you here?" The young girl waited. "One more time.

Phillip, remember me? I'm the one from the forest in Willow Glen, me and my dog Sadie."

In the distance, a small little light could be seen. "Annie, do you see that?"

"Yes, I do. I think it's Phillip." Annie grew excited.

The light got closer until it finally reached the two young children. "Oh, Phillip. It's you." Annie could barely contain her joy. "We're trapped. We fell in a trunk and we landed in a forest and bushes tried to grab us and Sam became alive and Ornoth and Fergus saved us and flew us here, and …" The words tumbled out.

"Wait. Ornoth and Fergus? Why didn't you say so? And how do you know my name?" The creature replied.

"Yes, Ornoth and Fergus. They said they were your friends," said Sam.

"Ornoth and Fergus are very good friends of the pixies. And who might you be?" The creature approached the boy.

"I'm Sam. I'm a friend of Annie's," Sam said with a shaky voice.

"Again, how do you know my name?" The pixie sounded angry.

"You know me, Phillip. Remember? I'm Annie. I met you near Willow Glen. I was with my dog Sadie."

"Willow Glen? Never heard of it. I never met you before and if you'd been in this forest, you and your dog would've been grabbed by the Black Thatcher." The flying pixie was not acting very friendly.

"But I found a crystal. Right after I met you. See?" Annie held out her crystal.

The creature examined the shiny shard. "You took a crystal from my cave?" He sounded alarmed.

"No, I found it outside. It wasn't in the cave, honest," said Annie, continuing her story. "Sam was dead, but I could see him as long as I was holding the crystal."

"Of course. That's because he was in between blinks," the creature said matter-of-factly.

"I don't understand," Annie said.

"If your friend was dead, he was in between blinks. That's where you go when you aren't here. The crystal lets you see what's in between." The pixie put the crystal in his pocket.

"Wait. That's my stone. May I have it back?" Annie held out her hand.

"It's not your stone. You stole it," Phillip snapped.

"Oh please, I found it outside of your cave. Please let me have it back," Annie pleaded.

Phillip gazed down at the piece of purple stone. "Alright. But you must promise to not give it to another soul." The winged pixie dropped the crystal into Annie's hand. "If Ornoth and Fergus trust you, then I trust you too."

"Thank you, Phillip. I will keep it safe, I promise," said Annie, her voice filled with relief.

"I will be on my way, now." The pixie changed back into a small orb of light.

"Wait. Please don't leave," Sam yelled. "Fergus brought us here. Ornoth had a map and said that the pixies could help us," Sam said in desperation.

Phillip snapped back to full form. "Hmmm. That is true. We do help our friends, but what kind of help do you need?"

"The Black Thatcher tried to get us," Sam remarked.

"And you escaped?" The pixie seemed shocked.

"Ornoth saved us or we would now be brambled, I'm sure," Sam remarked.

Phillip scratched his chin, as though in deep thought. "Since you escaped from The Black Thatcher, he knows you are in his forest," Phillip responded. "You are very lucky that you weren't brambled. The Black Thatcher cursed this forest many years ago and I have lost many friends to his evil brambles. I'm surprised you are standing here before me. Not many escape his vines," Phillip said sadly.

"Is this forest the same as the one where I first met you?" Annie asked.

"Since I have never met you before, I can't answer that. You are a peculiar creature, asking me such things. Why would you say we've met when we haven't?" Phillip appeared confused. "Wait here. I will be back soon." Phillip changed back into an orb and flew down the tunnel.

Annie turned to Sam and whispered. "I swear he is the same Phillip. Why doesn't he remember?"

"Do you think it's because the future hasn't happened yet?" Sam's question made sense.

"Why of course. That's got to be it. No wonder he didn't know why I knew his name. But Sam, don't you see? If this is the same forest where you and I met, there was no Black Thatcher there," said Annie with excitement.

"I hope you're right," replied Sam, sounding optimistic. "Maybe we will get back home."

CHAPTER ELEVEN

The tunnel curved and twisted as Phillip flew along its corridor. Arriving at his destination, Phillip transformed back into his full pixie self. "Gather round. Gather round." His voice echoed through the massive cavern. Bits of light started approaching the now standing pixie. "Hurry now. We have work to do," instructed Phillip.

"We have been sent some children, some human children." The sound of gasps and muttered voices grew loud. "Ornoth and Fergus sent them here. We need to help them get back home." Phillip gazed over the dozens of pixies who now stood before him, in their full form selves. "The Black Thatcher probably knows they are here by now, so we all must proceed with caution. We need to get them safely back to their home. Do I have any volunteers?" Phillip didn't see any takers.

"The last time we left the cave, the Black Thatcher was waiting for us. How will we be safe?" A pixie shouted out.

"These children say they come from another time. If what they say is true, there is only one person who can help them," Phillip stated. He heard a loud gasp.

"You mean Sylvia of the Shadows?" A shaky voice could be heard.

"I'm afraid so. She knows the spells that are needed. We can protect the children here, in the caves, but outside of here, they will need something much more powerful. Who will help?" Phillip's eyes moved over the many faces of his friends and family of pixies.

"I will," said a pixie with a small voice.
"Thomas? Splendid." Phillip smiled at the young pixie, not much older than the children. "Anyone else?"

"If Thomas goes, I must go," announced Thomas's father.

"And I will go," another pixie yelled out.

"Me too," said yet another.

The voices continued until there were at least thirty pixies ready to help the young humans reach their next destination.

"I am so proud of you. If we don't help our forest friends, we don't deserve our wings. Ornoth and Fergus care about these children so it is the right thing that we should help them," Phillip commented.

The pixies changed into their orb forms and floated towards the children, their flickering lights resembling a swarm of fireflies. Phillip led the way. "Follow me. Stay together now," shouted the head pixie.

The children came into view. They were seated on the stone path, the light from their torches losing strength. Phillip and the other pixies transformed into their body forms. "We're here. The most courageous of the pixies have volunteered to help you," the head pixie explained. Phillip saw the questioning look on the boy's face. "Is something wrong?" Phillip asked.

"I thought you'd have someone our size. You all are so small. How can you help us?" Sam replied.

"Size is not what is going to help here," Phillip replied. "Don't you trust us?"

"I mean, I meant to say, uh…" Sam stumbled on his words.

"You meant to say you don't think a bunch of small pixies can help you." Phillip stood firmly planted, his hands on his hips. "Let me tell you something. You obviously don't know what you are dealing with. It is black magic that the Black Thatcher has cursed upon this forest. You have no power over it. We don't either, other than to stay down here, hidden in our caves. You are safe as long as you are here with us, but the danger comes after you leave," Phillip warned.

The head pixie noticed that Sam had lowered his head, appearing to be ashamed. It was about time the boy started listening. This was a dangerous situation and Phillip knew that his group of pixies were putting their own lives in danger to help these children.

"I'm not sure what Ornoth and Fergus had in mind. Perhaps they thought we could hide you here forever," Phillip remarked. "But if you want to go home, back to your Willow Glen, then we need help from someone else."

Annie pleaded, "But I thought you could take us home. Phillip, you lived near my family's farm. Can't we go there?"

"Again, silly girl, I don't know what you are talking about. We will take you to Sylvia. She will know what to do." Phillip turned and faced the pixies. "I need some of you in front and some behind the children. Don't let them out of your sight. Even though the Black Thatcher can't come into the caves, he might have tricks up his sleeve. Let me know if you notice anything unusual." The pixies all nodded and then changed into their orb selves, all except Phillip. Bits of light fluttered around the children.

"What should we do?" Sam asked.

"You can leave your torches. We will provide the light. Follow me." Phillip moved slowly and carefully through the tunnel. He hoped that his idea was going to work.

"Ouch!" Annie shouted as her foot stumbled in a hole.
"Watch out for holes," Phillip remarked.

"Now you tell me," the girl whined. "I think I twisted my ankle."
Phillip told everyone to stop while he attended to the girl's injury. "Looks fine to me."

"It doesn't feel finc. Look. I can't even stand on it." Annie winced in pain.

"We can't stay here, or we won't reach Sylvia before dark." Phillip assembled his pixies and gave them instructions. Six of them changed into solid form and lifted Annie up, creating a chair with their arms. He was frustrated that these children seemed so clumsy.

"You are heavy," Thomas, one of the younger pixies commented to Annie.

"I'm sorry," Annie apologized. "I should've been more careful."

"We need to get going. Time is being wasted," Phillip barked to the group.

Sam had removed the rope tied around Annie. "Relax. At least you don't have to walk. I'm getting pretty tired."

"You humans sure complain a lot," Phillip grumbled. "Continue this way. We should get there soon."

The group kept pace and finally reached the end of the tunnel. Phillip was glad to see that it was still daylight. A hole led up to the ground above.

"Thomas, you go see what's above, but keep your glow down. The rest of you, raise energy for the shield. We will mesh the children to get them safely to Sylvia's cottage," Phillip instructed.

"Mesh? What are you going to do to us?" Sam asked.

"It's like a spider web but it's made of pixie dust and energy. It will protect you until you reach Sylvia. You will be safe once you get there." Phillip hoped the children would not panic when the web stuck to their bodies.

"What about you and the other pixies? Will you also be protected?" Sam sounded concerned.

"We won't be going with you. We can't mesh ourselves since we would not be able to fly." Phillip waited for Thomas to return.

"So why did you bring so many if you weren't planning on going with us?" Sam was now worried.

"The more pixies we have, the more energy can form your mesh. Your worry will only inhibit the mesh from working. I suggest you relax." Phillip couldn't understand why this boy child was so challenging.

"Sam, Phillip is trying to help. You need to trust him." Annie tried talking to her friend. "Take some deep breaths. That always helps me when I'm afraid."

"I'm not afraid," Sam whined.

"Sam, you sure aren't being very cooperative. Let Phillip explain. Phillip, how does this mesh work? How will we get to Sylvia's if you aren't going with us?" Annie trusted Phillip.

"You will float, of course." Phillip wondered why these humans asked such silly questions.

"Float? How are we going to float?" Sam asked, fear in his voice.

"The mesh is full of pixie dust and pixie energy. Have you not wondered how we turn into orbs?" Phillip offered an explanation.

"Yes, I did wonder. I figured it was fairy magic or something," Sam retorted.

"Fairy? We are not fairies," Phillip shouted with disgust.

"I'm sorry. What do you have against fairies?" Sam asked.

"What if I said you were just like a troll? You have two arms and two legs and you can't fly," Phillip snapped back at the stupid human boy. How dare he compare the pixies to fairies. Fairies are delicate and sensitive, healie-feelie and all that stuff. Pixies were rugged and sensible.

"I'm not a troll. They're ugly and hairy and have huge feet." Sam didn't like the comparison.

"Fairies are not like us. They are special in their own way, but we are pixies. Our abilities are much different," Phillip explained.

"I'm sorry. I didn't know. I won't call you that again. But can you tell me, how are we going to get to Sylvia's?" Sam sounded desperate.

Phillip decided to show a demonstration. He picked up a stone. "See this?"

"Sure. It's right there in your hand," Sam replied.

"Watch." Phillip closed his eyes and soon little specs of dust began to swirl. They sparkled and spun, faster and faster. The dust then circled the stone and a mesh resembling a spider's web stuck to its surface. Slowly, the round rock lifted from Phillip's hand, floating in mid-air.

Sam's eyes grew large.

"Now watch." Phillip lowered his hand and the stone remained floating. He pointed his finger and directed it towards the other side of the tunnel. The rock floated gently, still wrapped in the mesh, in whatever direction Phillip pointed. "This is what the mesh will do. Once you are meshed, I will stand at the cave entrance and concentrate on where you need to go. The mesh can pick up my thoughts and will float you towards your destination."

"That's amazing," Annie remarked. "Why can't you direct us home then?"

"That is a good question. I guess I would have to be able to picture your home in my head, and since you come from the future, it doesn't work the same." Phillip scratched his head, trying to imagine the possibilities. "Sylvia of the Shadows works all types of magic. If anyone can get you home, she can," said Phillip with confidence.

Thomas returned. "I couldn't see anything other than trees. There were no bushes in sight."

"Oh good. Looks like the Black Thatcher hasn't discovered your whereabouts then. Time to get everyone focusing," instructed

Phillip to the group of pixies. They all closed their eyes, folded down their wings, and joined hands. They hummed in unison. The dust swirled, like with the stone. It got larger and spun faster, forming a fine sticky mesh in its center. The mesh moved towards the children and encircled them, then adhered to their bodies like a fine silk glove.

"I can barely feel it," Annie spoke out.

"Me neither," Sam replied.

The pixies continued creating mesh, the younger ones collapsing when their energy ran out. Fortunately, there were enough of them to get the job done.

The children lifted off their feet and were soon midair, on their backs. "Everyone, concentrate and focus on Sylvia's cottage. This is where the children need to go," Phillip shouted to the group. They hummed, concentrating on their assignment. The children floated easily out the exit of the cave, hovering above the shrubs. Their reclined bodies, now cocooned in mesh, moved towards the dense forest. A sparkling pixie dust cloud was transporting them directly to Sylvia's home deep in the woods.

CHAPTER TWELVE

Annie wondered how far it was to Sylvia's cabin. She gazed over at Sam. He looked like he had been caught in a spider's web. She assumed her cocoon looked the same. Every time she hit a tree, the mesh bounced like a balloon. She wanted to talk to Sam and wondered if he could hear her.

"Sam. Can you hear me?" Annie shouted.

"Yes, loud and clear," Sam replied.

Annie was relieved that she could still speak to Sam. She felt the vial tucked safely in her pocket. "Still there," she thought. "Sam, do you still have your vial?"

"Yes, safe and sound," the boy replied.

In the distance, a cottage was barely visible. "Look, over there. I wonder if that's Sylvia's house?" Annie asked. She pushed her weight to one side to see if she could guide the bubble, but it had a mind of its own. Annie figured Phillip was driving the bubbles by using his mind.

"Look Annie. I think we're here," Sam yelled, his voice excited.

The meshed children floated up to the doorstep then were gently set down. The two young humans climbed out of the mesh and found themselves on the front steps of a small, wooden cottage. Smoke billowed from the chimney.

"Looks like someone is home," Sam remarked.

Annie examined the quaint building. It had a small oak door, barely her height. Moss covered the outer walls and the roof was thatched. The four-paned windows were curtained. "I saw a curtain move," Annie exclaimed

"I'm going to knock." Sam pulled up the large claw knocker and pounded it three times against the door.

The door swung open and there stood a short, stooped woman, her long gray hair dangling halfway down her back. Her clothing appeared old and worn. Her face was wrinkled and her steel blue eyes squinted, almost appearing closed. She had on woolen slippers. A weathered shawl was wrapped around her shoulders. "Come in. Come in. Don't stand out there in the cold and damp. I've been expecting you."

The children slowly walked inside, greeted by the smell of a savory soup. "You're just in time for supper. Are you hungry? When I received the message from the pixies, I figured I'd better have food ready. I know children eat a lot."

"I'm hungry," Sam said, his belly constantly growling for food.

"You're always hungry, now that you are alive again," Annie retorted. "You must be Sylvia. We are so happy to finally be here."

The old woman smiled. "Yes, I am Sylvia. How did you like being meshed?"

"It felt strange," Sam replied.

Sylvia brushed something from Sam's hair. "You still have pixie dust on you. It will wear off soon." The old woman laughed, then shuffled towards the table. "Here. Sit down. I will dish you up some soup."

Annie pulled out a chair and sat down. "We have many questions Sylvia. We hope you can help us."

"I will do what I can but first, we must eat." Sylvia grinned a big smile, her teeth desperately needing repair. She placed three large bowls of soup on the table. "Please eat. You don't want it to get cold."

"This is delicious. What's in it?" Annie barely thought of her visit to Phillip and her promise not to eat meat.

"Carrots, potatoes, and a bit of rabbit." Sylvia didn't even look up as she slurped her soup.

"Rabbit?" Annie put her spoon down.

"Do you have a problem eating rabbit?" Sylvia asked.

"It's just that, I promised…" Annie struggled with her secret. "I guess I will tell you. Before we fell into the trunk, I found a cave, a hidden cave. I met a pixie there named Phillip, the same Phillip who helped us get here to your cottage, only he doesn't remember. Oh, it's all so confusing." Annie hoped Sylvia could follow along.

"I made a promise," Annie said, as tears formed in her eyes. Sylvia gazed at the young girl. "Go on."

"I was there with my dog, Sadie, and we were having a picnic. Phillip saw that I had meat in my basket, and he got so upset. He said that eating meat was a horrible thing to do, that the animals in the forest were friends and we shouldn't eat them. I made a promise that I wouldn't eat meat again."

"You silly child." Sylvia laughed. "Pixies don't eat meat, but you aren't a pixie. You're a human."

"What does that have to do with it?" Annie asked, wiping the tears from her face.

"When humans were created, oh so long ago, they needed nourishment to survive. There were things they were given to eat - berries, mushrooms, roots, flowers, leaves, and animals." Sylvia became serious. "The animals were to be hunted, but then blessed. Humans did not take this gift for granted."

"But the animals. What about the pain?" Annie's voice shook.

"Before the animal was killed, a blessing was said to take any pain or suffering away. This was important. The same is true now. Before you eat, you should always say a blessing to honor the animal. It gives their soul peace and thanks them for their sacrifice." Sylvia bowed her head.

"I didn't think animals had souls," Annie remarked.

"Of course they do," said Sylvia.

"So, it's alright for me to eat rabbit?" Annie would love if she could rid herself of this guilt.

"Yes, dear child. Say thank you to the spirit of the rabbit. He will continue his journey in another realm. His flesh isn't needed there." Sylvia again began eating.

"Oh thank you, Sylvia. I was in a terrible argument with my father. He was so upset I no longer wanted to eat meat." She then remembered her parents' fight.

"Eat up. Your soup is getting cold." Sylvia emptied her bowl with a final slurp. "I see Sam is already finished. Feel free to have a second bowl."

"Thank you. Don't mind if I do." Sam headed for the pot and refilled his bowl.

Annie realized Sam hadn't even been listening to the confession she had made to Sylvia. It seemed that all he cared about now was his stomach.

"May this soup nourish my body and may all who gave their lives be rewarded in heaven." Annie wondered if this prayer would work once she got home. It would make her father so happy if she ate meat again. Still, the thought of eating anything that could look into her eyes was more than she could handle.

"That is a nice blessing. See? It's not so hard," said Sylvia with a smile.

After their meal, Annie helped wash the dishes and then went into the cozy room to enjoy the warmth of the fireplace. There were shelves lining the walls. Annie squinted trying to read the titles. "Where did you get so many books?"

"They find their way here from different travelers. Do you enjoy reading?" Sylvia pulled a book off the shelf. "I bet you might like this one. It's about a girl and her dog. I have many others, some for children's eyes and some much more mysterious."

"I love dogs. I miss my dog so much. May I borrow the book, the one about the dog?" Annie's emotions took hold.

Sylvia lightly touched Annie's hair. "Oh sweet child, why didn't you bring her with you? Dogs are most welcome here," the old woman said.

"Sylvia, you need to understand. We aren't here by choice. We fell here, through time. Annie's dog is back home, in Willow Glen," Sam explained.

Annie realized that Sam was finally paying attention to their conversation.

"Yes, Phillip messaged me what happened." Sylvia leaned forward, her gentle eyes now sparkling from the glow of the candles. "But I believe there will be much more to your story. There is so much more than meets the eye."

CHAPTER THIRTEEN

Sylvia's cottage was warm, and the evening turned to night. Sam wondered what Sylvia meant about there being more to the story. Did Sylvia know something she wasn't sharing?

The old woman turned to Sam. "Perhaps you can start at the beginning and tell me everything. Maybe Phillip left something out." Sylvia's curiosity peaked.

Sam told the story of what little he remembered of his life, then of his death. He told of his endless years in the forest waiting for someone to take him to heaven, about meeting Annie, the crystal, and the trunk. He described how it felt to be alive again, and of being saved by Ornoth. "So, you see, we only want to go home although I don't think I want to be dead again. Phillip believed you could help us. Can you?"

Sylvia summarized, "Sam, you're saying you are eleven years old but have been dead for over a hundred years. You lived in a forest waiting for your mother who never came. And you missy, are also eleven, live on a farm near a place called Willow Glen, have a dog named Sadie, and your parents aren't your real parents." The old woman paced the room.

"Uh huh," Annie and Sam both nodded.

The forest woman continued, "Annie, you met Phillip, but promised never to reveal his secret cave, then found a crystal on your way home. The crystal allowed you to see Sam when no one else could. You fell into a trunk at a church, landed in the forest, and were saved by Ornoth from being brambled. You then realized that Sam was now a living breathing boy. Fergus saved you from the Black Thatcher and took you to the pixie's cave where you met Phillip again, only he didn't remember you this time. He and the other pixies meshed you and sent you here. Have I missed anything?" Sylvia took a sip of tea and heaved a heavy sigh.

"Nope. That's pretty much it," Sam exclaimed, amazed at how crazy the story sounded now that he heard it out loud. "It sounds hard to believe, doesn't it?" Sam worried that Sylvia might think he made it all up.

"First of all Sam, everyone who dies goes to the realm in between blinks. Everyone. For some reason, you felt a need to stay in the forest. There is no other explanation. We will figure this out. It could be that you had unfinished business, maybe something you didn't even know about," the wise woman explained.

Sam tilted his head. "Unfinished business?"

"Sometimes our souls have a purpose that we have forgotten about. If your soul wasn't ready for its journey to the afterworld, it may have decided to finish what still needed to be done." Sylvia scratched her chin.

"Limbo? So being a ghost is being in limbo?" Sam questioned.

"Exactly." The woman patted Sam's head. "I know not of this place called Willow Glen. To get you back to somewhere I have no knowledge of, would be a significant challenge. I could not guarantee you, dear boy, that returning you to where you came from would not also make you dead again." The woman's voice softened. "It is possible that you would go to the land in between blinks, once you were returned."

Sam's face fell. "You aren't sure if you can help us?"

Sylvia took the children's hands. "Listen to me dear ones. I am called Sylvia of the Shadows. I live in the shadows so as not to be hit by sunlight. It would do a terrible thing to me. I can tell you no more about that other than there are many things in this forest, magical and mystical. It is an enchanted forest but also a cursed one. Do you know the difference?"

Annie replied. "Cursed is bad?"

"Yes. Let me explain. A long time ago, the forest came under an enchantment spell. I don't know from where, but those who lived here in this forest, fell under the enchantment. We didn't age any older than what we were at that time. We had all the food we needed. Time seemed to stop. The pixies, fairies, and even trolls, all learned to live in peace and harmony with the humans. Some of the animals changed, growing to unusual sizes and being able to speak human words, like Fergus. We were happy and all became friends." Sylvia stopped to take another sip of tea. "One day, something bad happened. Berry bushes took over the forest and choked out many of the trees. Our friends disappeared. Those of us who had been young for many years, turned old and gray. Many perished." Sylvia's eyes became distant.

Annie reached for the old woman's hand. "I'm sorry. That must've been very hard for you."

"The worst part was losing my friends. One day I was happy, free to go out in the forest. We would have great parties. The pixies loved to dance, and Ornoth would play his flute. Fergus would spin around wildly, his feathers flying. The fairies and pixies would sing and many others from the forest would join in. We all had such wonderful times." Sylvia's eyes filled with tears.

"Where did they all go?" Sam asked.

"The pixies went underground. They have caves and found safety there. The fairies had to return to their own realm and could no longer visit here, except when they were summoned for those things only they can do. Ornoth and Fergus had to stay in their cottage, although Fergus visits when he can. He can fly high enough to stay above the forest. I lost track of all the rest." The old woman's voice filled with sadness.

"Is the Black Thatcher the one who broke the enchantment?" Annie asked.

"Probably, but no one really knows for sure. We do know that the Black Thatcher is responsible for all those who are missing. He brambled them." Sylvia's voice filled with emotion. "My friends are all gone, trapped in his wicked berries. And me, getting older and older. I have a potion that keeps me alive, but one day I know I will die. It's only a matter of time."

"There must be something we can do. How can we put the enchantment back? Aren't you a witch? Can't you reverse it?" Sam said with urgency. He'd been told stories about witches. They practiced magic and could put spells on things. He always thought they were evil, though, and Sylvia didn't seem evil.

"Who told you witches were evil? Far from it," said the woman, laughing.

"Phillip said you were able to do magic," Annie replied.

"I have been taught how to use the elements of nature. We all have that ability," said Sylvia. "Listen, children, you have been through a lot and there is much on your minds. Let's get some sleep and we can talk more about this in the morning."

"That sounds like a perfect idea." Sam's face lit up. "But first, I need to use your loo."

"Loo? What is a loo?" Sylvia asked, a puzzled look on her face.

Sam wondered how to politely explain the situation. "I've eaten a lot and drank too much tea. My body needs to get rid of some of it."

"Oh, dear child. That is what you mean." Sylvia laughed a big hearty laugh. "Here, down the hall. Let me show you." Sylvia led the boy to a small closet-sized room in the corner of the house. She showed him two buckets, one with a seat and one that was filled with sand. The elderly woman pointed to one of the buckets. "You sit on that one then pour sand over the top when you're done. I will empty it in the morning. If it's liquid, it goes in that bucket." Sylvia pointed to a lidded container in the corner.

Sam sighed in relief. It was embarrassing talking about these things, especially to girls. He remembered his experience at Ornoth's cabin. "This is way better than what Ornoth had. He gave us an enchanted stick that we had to take outside, but we only had three minutes to do our business or risked getting brambled," Sam commented with a chuckle.

"That's why I have inside facilities," remarked Sylvia, followed by a large bellowing laugh. "No point in going outside if you do your business inside."

Sam waited until he knew the woman was gone. He sat down on the bucket and thought about all that had happened. There was something about this grandmotherly lady that he liked. She wasn't scary and she acted concerned and caring. He felt like there was something she wasn't saying though. He finished his business and poured in the sand like Sylvia said to do.

"I feel much better." Sam rejoined Annie and Sylvia. "Annie, it's not bad. There's a bucket and it has a seat and it's indoors." He was happy to see Annie smile.

"Here, sit in front of the fire and get warm. The night will be cold. Come enjoy the fire while it's still burning. I will tell you my ideas." Sylvia grabbed a thick shawl then rocked in a worn rocking chair. She pulled out some yarn and knitting needles and began knitting while she rocked. The fire's embers gave off a soft glow and the room was toasty. "This is lovely. I haven't had company in a long time." Sylvia's smile was warm.

Sam sat down in a big green stuffed chair near the fireplace, leaving the smaller blue chair for his friend. Annie returned from the closet loo and got comfortable in the chair left for her next to Sam.

"What are you knitting Sylvia?" Annie asked.

"A pair of socks. Mine are worn, and winter will be here soon." She held up her foot to show the hole that had been repaired several times. "Yarn is hard to come by, so I have to make things last." Sylvia counted the stitches in her head as she knitted.

"My mother knits. She made this sweater for me." Annie turned to show Sylvia the intricate design.

"Your mother must love you very much to make such a fancy sweater for you." Sylvia admired the beautiful design.

Annie's eyes filled with tears. "But she isn't even my mother. Oh Sylvia, where did I come from? I don't even know who my real parents are."

Sylvia put her knitting down and moved over to the sobbing child. She gently cradled her in her arms, rocking back and forth. "Listen, sweet girl, a mother's love isn't dependent on flesh and blood. It's here, in the heart." The woman placed her hand over Annie's chest. "I'm sure you are loved greatly."

"That's what my parents said, that I was special and that they loved me more than any parents could possibly love their child. They had lost three babies, all from the same type of illness. They wanted a family and when they met me at the orphanage, I was the answer to their prayers," Annie recalled. "The children at the orphanage said I was stolen by fairies and that they are the ones who put me in the forest to be found. I never believed in fairies but now I know there are many unbelievable things that are very real."

"I think we need to be focusing on other things. What can we do, Sylvia?" Sam changed the subject. He wanted to know how they were going to get home.

"When you were telling me your story, Sam, I kept seeing a woman in my head. I have seen her before." Sylvia closed her eyes. "You said after you died, you were not able to find your mother and wondered why you weren't joined with her in heaven."

"Yes, that's right," Sam replied.

"What if she never died?" Sylvia asked.

"My mother must be dead by now. It's been over a hundred years. She would be at least 130 years old. It's not possible for her to still be alive." Sam pulled off his cap and ran his fingers through his hair. "I waited for her. She should've come for me, you know, once she was an angel." Sam's grief washed over him.

"Do you remember what your mother looked like?" Sylvia asked the sullen boy.

"Of course I do. She was so beautiful. She had brown hair, like mine. It was long, almost to her waist, but she wore it up twisted around her head. She had brown eyes, like mine. Her fingers were long, and she'd play the piano. She loved to sing to me," said Sam, remembering.

"And her name? Do you remember her name?" The old woman inquired.

"Martha. Her name was Martha Sullivan," Sam replied.

"And your father? Do you remember him?" Sylvia had more questions.

"No. I never met my father. My mother said he died before I was born. Why are you asking me these questions?" Sam was confused.

"I am what you might call, a seer. I see things in the past, in the present, and in the future. Sometimes visions come through blurry, but sometimes they are very clear. If I gaze in this black dish of water, sometimes images appear." Sylvia reached for her scrying bowl and peered intently into it. "I see a woman, just as you described. I see her sitting in a room. She is dressed in a blue dress and has long brown hair. She is reading by candlelight."

"That could be anyone. What makes you think it could be my mother?" Sam questioned the old woman, wondering why she was telling him this.

"She is calling out a name. Sammy, my sweet Sammy. I am so sorry. And she is humming a melody. It sounds like this." Sylvia hummed the song.

Sam sat quietly, his eyes closed, his thoughts returning to a time long ago when he was a very young boy. "Sammy. My mother used to call me Sammy. And that song, she'd sing it to me when she put me to bed. Where is she? Where is this woman?" Sam pleaded.

"Sam, do you think it really could be her?" Annie reached for Sam's hand.

"I don't know. What else can you see?" Sam wanted so much to believe.

"Remember I told you I'd seen a woman before? She was this woman, this woman I am seeing now." The old woman kept her eyes closed. "I don't know why I hadn't remembered this before. But she was here, right here in this forest. She told a story like yours, about how she had fallen through time and didn't know how to return home. She found my cottage and knocked upon my door. She sat right where you are sitting now." Sylvia tried to remember all the details. "She told me of a son, a boy who had died. She had been in the church and had gone to find candles. Somehow, she stumbled in the dark and found herself spinning and tumbling, much like yourselves." Sylvia's memory grew stronger.

"My mother was here? No wonder she didn't come for me. She couldn't. She was trapped here. Is she still alive?" Sam asked anxiously. Could it be possible? Was his mother alive?

"I see her being still alive, Sam. I think she was enchanted like the rest of us which is why she didn't die. But I also must warn you." Sylvia's look changed.

"What? What must I be warned about?" Sam could barely contain himself.

"She isn't aging like the rest of us. Even though the enchantment ended, she is still as young as the day she found herself here." Sylvia gazed into the air, her visions becoming clearer. "She is imprisoned. She is in a cell. I am so sorry, Sam, but I believe she is being held by the Black Thatcher."

At this news, Sam jumped up, face red with anger, fists clenched. "I must find this Black Thatcher. I will rescue my mother. He can't stop me."

"Wait young man. Let me finish. There is more. Sit down, sit down," Sylvia said with a calm voice. "As I said, your mother is alive and doesn't appear to be aging. Do you know what that means?"

"No. What does that mean?" Sam was now more confused than ever.

"If she arrived here when you died, that was over a hundred years ago. And if she looks the same now as she did then, and the enchantment spell has been broken for many years, there is something else keeping her young. My guess is that the Black Thatcher has done something to her." Sylvia pondered, grabbing her chin and focusing on more visions.

A horrified look came over Sam's face. "You mean she..."

"She must be drinking the bramble elixir," Annie gasped as she spoke the words.

"My mother wouldn't do that. There is no way. My mother was kind and gentle," Sam shouted.

"I don't think she has a choice. The Black Thatcher must've told her she'd die unless she drank the juice. Maybe she doesn't even know where it's coming from," Sylvia said solemnly.

Sam didn't feel well. His stomach churned and wretched. He ran into the small closet room and the contents of his stomach spewed out of his mouth into the bucket. "Mother, you're alive but you're bewitched. Have I lost you all over again?" Sam crumpled to the floor and felt more pain than he had ever felt. When he regained himself, he walked back into the sitting room and joined Sylvia and Annie.

"So, what do we do now? How can we find Sam's mother?" Annie asked.

"I have an idea and it involves a friend of yours," Sylvia commented.

"Who? We don't know anyone here," Sam replied.

"Of course you do. You have made many friends since arriving here. We need to get a message to Fergus. I believe he will be the one to help us now," Sylvia said.

"But how will we do that? Won't the Black Thatcher see us in the forest?" Sam sounded frightened. "Fergus is with Ornoth and that is quite far, I believe."

"We aren't going into the forest." Sylvia peered back into her scrying bowl and began chanting, her hands circling over the swirling shapes that had formed.

Smooth as silk and black as night,
I summon you oh bird of flight,
May you fly above the trees,
and come to us we ask you, please.

Fergus, Fergus, friend so dear,
Fly to us, we need you here,
Only you can do this deed,
Please help us find the truth we need.

"There. That should do it," remarked Sylvia as she returned the bowl to its stand. As she walked towards the children, she commented. "A little magic I have up my sleeves."

"It looked like there was a storm in the water. What kind of magic was that?" Annie asked.

"It's called scrying. Sometimes I can see things in the water. Other times I use it to send messages, like now." The woman sat down and gathered up her knitting. "Now we wait. I think it's time we go to bed. We have much to do tomorrow. I haven't stayed up this late in a long time."

Sam sat quietly, watching the fireplace embers die. Annie was already asleep in the chair, and Sylvia had shuffled off to her room. Sam tried to stay awake but his eyes grew heavy and he knew he should get some rest. All those years of wishing he could sleep and now he wanted to stay awake. He thought about his mother as he drifted away to his dreams.

CHAPTER FOURTEEN

Morning arrived and Sam stirred. "It's very cold in here." Sam pulled the blanket around him. "Annie. Wake up. It's morning."

Annie's eyes opened and she sat up, then rubbed her eyes. "Why did you wake me? I was having such a wonderful dream." Realizing where she was, she looked at Sam. "Where's Sylvia?"

Sun was streaming in the windows but there was no sound coming from within the cottage. The fireplace embers had died out and the floor felt so cold. Sam walked towards Sylvia's bedroom and pushed the door slightly open. He saw Sylvia on the bed, her eyes closed. "Sylvia? Are you awake?" There was no answer. Sam walked closer. He looked at the woman's face, but something was different. "Sylvia." Sam tried shaking her. The woman didn't move. "Annie. I don't think Sylvia is breathing. Come quick," Sam shouted in a panicked tone.

Annie ran into the room and approached the bed. "Oh Sam. Do you think she's dead?" Annie's face was horrified.

"I don't know. What should we do?" Sam said, his voice shaking.

"We need to get help but we can't go out into the forest. Sam. I'm scared," Annie shouted.

"Do you think Fergus will come?" Annie asked through her trembling voice.

"Right now, I think we need to light a fire before we freeze. Come help me get some logs." Sam regained some composure and headed for the porch. He opened the door to grab some logs that he'd noticed the night before. "Here. Put these in the fireplace. There should be kindling in the bucket."

Annie took the wood and placed it in the fireplace. "Now what do I do?"

"Light it. There should be matches on the hearth." Annie figured out what to do and soon there was a crackling fire in the fireplace.

"Good job. It's already feeling warmer in here," Sam commented. He was glad that Annie was smart and didn't need lots of instructions. After all, he couldn't do everything. He'd been out of practice for a very long time. He liked feeling useful again. For so long, he'd been a wisp, a mere portion of a human. It felt good to be alive.

"Why did Sylvia have to die?" Annie's head dropped.

"I don't know. I hope Fergus got her message." Sam waited on the porch and felt his feet on worn boards. The scent of fir trees filled his nose. If he wasn't so scared, he could be happy right now. He looked up and saw a black streak coming towards him. "Oh no! The Black Thatcher has found us." Sam's heart sank.

CHAPTER FIFTEEN

Ornoth bit into a biscuit with one gnarled hand as he moved the red wooden button with his other hand. "Your turn."

"I knew you were going to do that," said Fergus as he picked up a black button and jumped two red pieces on the checkerboard. He had been living here for almost as long as he could remember. Beating Ornoth at checkers was no easy feat.

"I didn't see that. You are one sneaky bird." Ornoth pushed his chair back then went to prepare more moss tea. He tapped his head with his hand and shook it hard. "I think that must be it, my head wasn't cleared." The old troll offered his usual excuse.

"Do you think the children made it safely? I haven't heard any alarms from the pixies," Fergus remarked. Sam and Annie had been on his mind ever since he'd dropped them off at the pixie cave. He could only hope that they didn't encounter any unexpected company.

"I'm sure they are almost home by now. The pixies have never let us down," Ornoth replied. He placed a steaming cup of tea in front of Fergus and then went back for his own cup. "It was nice having company, wasn't it?" Ornoth's voice softened.

"We don't get many visitors. I wonder why they ended up here, in this forest and at this time?" Fergus had many questions. "My head is buzzing. Wait." Fergus fluffed up his wings and situated his body. "Ornoth, I think I'm picking up something." The buzz got stronger and stronger.

Ornoth set down his cup. "Who is it?"

"I'm not sure. It feels like it could be Sylvia. Why would she be contacting me? I haven't spoken to her in a long time." Fergus closed his dark, black eyes as he focused on the thoughts being sent. "Yes. Yes. Uh. Yes."

"What are you hearing?" Ornoth could barely contain himself.

"It's from Sylvia. She's sending a message. It sounds like it's an emergency. She needs my help. I need to go to her." Fergus jumped up and headed towards the door. He knew it must be serious. That's the only time Sylvia ever contacted him.

"Wait. You can't fly off like that. What if it's a trick. Are you sure it's Sylvia?" Ornoth asked in a suspicious tone.

"I can tell. It is from her. Her energy is unique. Don't worry. I will be fine. I know exactly where her cottage is, and I can fly over the forest to escape the Black Thatcher. I challenge you to another game of checkers when I return." Fergus tipped his wing to Ornoth and jumped out the door, hopping a few steps before flying up into the sky.

§ § §

"It's Fergus," Sam shouted, his voice sounding relieved. He had thought the large black creature was the Black Thatcher. "Oh Fergus, I am so happy to see you." Sam charged into Fergus's feathered chest.

"That's a strong greeting," Fergus uttered as he caught his breath. "I received Sylvia's message and got here as fast I could. I sure didn't expect to see you here." Fergus unruffled his feathers and entered the cabin. "Where's Sylvia?"

"Fergus, something terrible has happened to Sylvia." Sam closed the door behind them.

"What has happened? And why are you here? I thought the pixies would have found a way to get you home by now," asked Fergus.

"They didn't know how to help us so they meshed us and sent us here," Sam explained.

Annie flew into Fergus's feathers. "I am so glad you're here, Fergus. I am so frightened."

"Where's Sylvia?" Fergus asked.

"In the bedroom. We think she's dead," the young boy said sadly.

Fergus bounded towards the bedroom, then saw Sylvia's still body on the bed. He then noticed the window. He rushed to it and closed the curtain. "Was the curtain open when you found her?"

"Uh, I guess so. We hadn't noticed," Sam replied.

"Sylvia, sweet Sylvia of the Shadows. Oh children, she cannot be around sunlight. She must've forgotten to close the curtain before she went to bed." Fergus leaned over the old woman. It wasn't like her to forget such a thing. "Sylvia, can you hear me?" There was no reply. He bowed his head, a tear falling on the still woman's face. "I'm afraid she's gone."

Annie sobbed loudly. "We talked to her last night. She was fine. She was so kind to us. She saw Sam's mother in a vision. At least we think it was Sam's mother. That's why she called to you. She was scrying." Annie spoke rapidly, her words hardly making sense. "She can't be dead. Isn't there anything we can do?"

Fergus led the children out of the bedroom and closed the door. "I'm sorry. She's gone. I'm afraid the Black Thatcher's curse finally killed her."

"What curse?" Sam asked, fear flashing in his eyes.

The crow walked around the cottage and noticed that all the curtains were open. He knew then that Sylvia must've been focused on something important before going to bed. He didn't want to alarm the children but things had taken a turn for the worse.

CHAPTER SIXTEEN

Fergus led the children into the main room. He sat down in Sylvia's rocking chair, moving the half-finished socks to the floor. His thoughts went back to the many times he'd spent with the odd woman. Sylvia's story was tragic, but she had never let it stop her from doing all she could to protect those in the forest. He knew what must've happened to Sylvia. Her heart would've been heavy, feeling so much sadness for Sam and Annie. Her thoughts probably had been on how she could help them and not on closing her curtains. Even if she had remembered in the morning, it would've been too late. Fergus felt sad. Sylvia had been a good friend.

"Before I tell you about Sylvia, tell me what happened in the pixie caves?" Fergus was still puzzled about finding Annie and Sam here, far from the caves.

"Phillip found us but when we told him about trying to get home, he didn't know how to help us. He thought Sylvia would have a way. He meshed us," said Annie as she described what happened. "We were covered in sticky stuff and we floated and bounced off trees. It was the oddest feeling."

Fergus was surprised. He pictured the children floating and bouncing through the forest in giant bubbles, not something he thought Phillip would risk doing. "I am glad you arrived here safely however Phillip put you at great risk sending you out of the caves." Fergus leaned towards Sam and Annie. "Listen carefully. You are not safe here now that Sylvia is gone. We need a plan to get you out of this forest."

"But what about Sylvia? We can't leave her here," Annie said with concern.

"Please, tell us about the curse. Why did Sylvia die? She knew magic yet still she died. How could that be?" asked Sam.

Fergus knew the children needed to know the truth. He wasn't sure how much he should tell them. They were so young. "I must start at the beginning. Many years ago, there was a King who ruled over all these lands. He was a good King and took care of his people. Everyone worked hard and shared what they had so that no one went hungry. There were festivals and feasts. The King loved to dance and there would be music and laughter. It was a wonderful Kingdom. During one of the celebrations, a visitor arrived, claiming to come from a distant land. He bowed before the King and gave him a gift, a sword covered in jewels, with a golden hilt and a blade of great strength. The King was pleased with the beautiful gift and carried it proudly, showing it off to everyone he saw. The visitor loved the lands so much, he asked if he could stay in the castle. He knew many things and would be of great help to the King. Thrilled to have such an offer, the King gave the stranger a position within the realm. A year went by and then another. Soon the King had lost all interest in ruling, caring only for the sword and how special it made him feel." Fergus's eyes closed as he remembered the story. He had been a young crow then.

Fergus continued. "The visitor worked for the King but soon was advising the King how to rule. The King had great respect for this foreign visitor, this traveler who praised him at every turn. Thinking the visitor had great wisdom, the King took the visitor's advice and by royal decree, the people were ordered to turn over their crops, their livestock, and anything of value. If they refused, they would be thrown in the dungeon, or worse, hung from the gallows. The King became greedy and uncaring. Sadly, the people didn't know that their ruler had fallen under a spell and that the sword he adored carried black magic." Sam and Annie sat mesmerized by the story.

"What an awful King. How could he be so mean?" Annie asked.

"There is more to the story, Annie. One day, the King vanished. No one knew what had happened to him. The visitor took over and anyone who stood in his way was either imprisoned or killed. The people ran away into the forest, this forest... frightened of the man who had taken over the castle. They didn't know that he had also bewitched the forest. Thick thorny bushes grew where none had been before. Long winding vines began grabbing anyone who ventured into the forest and soon everyone who remained was brambled."

Sam gasped. "So, the Black Thatcher is this visitor? This person who killed the King?"

"No one knows for sure if the King was killed but he was never seen again. And yes, this visitor was the Black Thatcher," Fergus remarked.

Annie and Sam sat quietly and still, their faces showing disbelief.

"Sylvia was a brave woman. She had always helped the people with her herbs and tinctures. Her home was here, in this cottage in the forest. She cared for the people, providing remedies, and she attended to all the births, helping to bring babies into the world. The Black Thatcher came here and tried to bramble Sylvia. Her potions protected her from the brambles. The Black Thatcher was furious. He knew she needed to go into the forest to gather her herbs, so he placed a curse on her, more powerful than she was able to counter. He said that she must stay in the shadows forever or would die. If sunlight were to hit her, she would perish."

Annie gasped. "That's awful!"

Fergus's eyes closed as he remembered the time she had helped him after he'd fallen from a tree. His wing broken; she had cared for him until he could fly again.

"All this time she has had to stay inside?" Sam asked.

"She could venture outside at night or on stormy days when the clouds hid the sun." Fergus gazed down at the half-finished sock. "Sylvia was a wonderful woman. She saved many from the grasp of the Black Thatcher. Like Ornoth's cabin, Sylvia's cottage was safe from the Black Thatcher, but she did not have the magic that was needed to break the Black Thatcher's curse. It was more powerful than anything she had seen," Fergus commented.

"Why is Ornoth's cabin safe?" Annie asked.

Fergus rubbed his beak. "I can only tell you what Ornoth has told me. I met him when I was still a fledgling. He rescued me from the vines after I had flown too close. He protected me and said I was welcome to stay with him if I chose. How could I say no? I couldn't find my family and many of my friends, the rabbits, squirrels, deer and other animals in the forest, had all been brambled. We were all so frightened," explained Fergus.

"Ornoth became my family. I have been with him all these years. I have learned how to avoid the clutches of the Black Thatcher and I am able to bring food to Ornoth, so he doesn't have to leave the cabin except when he takes the stick to do his business." Fergus laughed at the thought.

"Sylvia uses buckets. It is much better," Annie replied.

"That seems much more dignified," remarked Fergus with a grin. "But to continue… Ornoth treated me like family and one day he decided to tell me what made his cabin safe. I am not sure I believe it, but it is the only answer I have ever been given."

"What? What is the answer?" Sam asked with apprehension.

"Ornoth said that the sword, the one with the jewels and the golden hilt, is buried beneath the cabin. It has magic. It has a protection spell." Fergus raised his wing as he spoke.

"Maybe we could find it?" Sam said with excitement. "How did he know it was buried? Maybe he stole it."

"He didn't steal it. Ornoth is a good and honest troll. He said it was given to him and he hid it beneath his cabin. That's all I know. But right now, I think we need to concentrate on getting you safely home. Sylvia's body needs tending. I will send for the fairies. There is a special ceremony they will do for her. Excuse me. I must go and pay my respects." Fergus got up from the chair and walked to the bedroom, closing the door behind him, tears filling his black onyx eyes.

Summoning fairies was tricky. Fergus knew where Sylvia kept her potions and herbs. "It must be here." He searched through the bottles and jars, boxes and bags. "Ah, here it is." Fergus grabbed a small bottle that had a purple swirling liquid inside. He took the bottle to Sylvia's bed then removed the lid.

"I hope I can remember the incantation," Fergus said to himself. He had only seen Sylvia summon the fairies once after the death of an infant she was trying to bring into the world. It was risky for the fairies to come here but he knew they would. It was an important ceremony that only they could perform.

Listen, listen, those of light,
Come here now on winged flight,
Sprinkle now with fairy dust,
What you will, what you must.

Fergus sprinkled drops of the purple liquid on Sylvia's still body. He knew the fairies would arrive quickly. He would have to say his good-byes now.

"Good-bye gentle lady. I will see you again one day. The children are safe with me. Thank you, sweet soul." A tear fell from Fergus's black eye.

A cloud of purple sparkly lights suddenly surrounded Sylvia's form. Fergus watched as the once solid woman turned to purple dust. She swirled into a column of light and then vanished, as though pulled through an invisible door. The fairies followed right behind.

"Wow," Sam uttered.

"I didn't know you were there." Fergus hadn't realized that the children had opened the door and entered the bedroom.

"She is gone. The fairies will help her cross to where her soul is to go, in between blinks," Fergus said to the children.

"You mean she's not going to heaven?" Sam asked.

"Sort of, Sam. She has been taken by the fairies. They help souls enter another realm after their bodies die. There are many words for heaven. It depends on what you believe," Fergus commented, tears still in his dark eyes.

"Maybe that's why I never went to heaven? Maybe there aren't any fairies in Willow Glen?" Sam scratched his head, although he remembered what Sylvia had told him. His soul might have unfinished business.

"Fairies are everywhere. There had to be another reason." Fergus wasn't sure why Sam was never taken.

"So, what do we do now?" Annie asked Fergus.

"I was summoned by Sylvia. I never found out what it is she wanted. Perhaps you can tell me?" Fergus looked at the children, obviously shaken from the tragic event.

"Oh, I know," Sam said eagerly. "Sylvia had a vision. She said she saw a woman in a room, like a cell. The woman looked like my mother and had called out the name Sammy. Sylvia thought this woman could be my mother."

"That would be odd. You said you had been dead for over a hundred years. How could your mother still be alive?" Fergus pondered.

"Sylvia said this woman was being forced to drink the bramble juice. That the Black Thatcher was keeping her alive." Sam's voice shook.

Annie spoke up. "Maybe you could fly to the castle, to where the Black Thatcher lives. If you find this woman and find out if she's Sam's mother, Sam could be reunited with her."

"I suppose I could fly to the castle, but I can't leave you two here alone." Fergus tried thinking of solutions. "You can't leave this cottage. It isn't safe. I am not strong enough to carry both of you and even if I was, how could I keep you safe? The Black Thatcher would sense you as soon as my feet touched the ground. And besides, how would I be able to even tell if the woman was your mother, or not? I would need you with me, Sam."

"I'll stay here. You can take Sam," Annie said. "And if it is his mother, you could leave him there."

"Would I have to drink bramble juice too?" Sam asked, his face twisted in disgust.

"No, no. That's not a good idea. We need to get this woman away from the castle." Fergus paced and paced in front of the fire, his black feathers glistening.

"We could trick him, lure him away from the castle like a distraction," Sam commented.

"He has spies. They would know." Fergus knew there must be a way to rescue the trapped woman.

"Maybe Phillip could help," Annie shouted out.

"Of course. Let's call Phillip," Sam said.

"The Pixies don't go near the castle," Fergus replied.

"But maybe they know a way to keep us safe so you can go," suggested Sam.

"I guess it's worth a try. Show me where Sylvia keeps her scrying bowl. I will try to contact Phillip that way." Fergus knew that he would have to use a different form of communication to get in touch with Phillip.

Sam showed Fergus where the bowl was. It still had water in it from when Sylvia had used it last. "Look, there is something still visible," Sam remarked.

Fergus peered into the bowl and a woman's image came into view. "Sam, come closer. Is this your mother?"

Sam gazed into the bowl and saw a young woman sitting on a wooden chair. She was knitting. "I'm not sure. It was so long ago when I last saw her."

"Look closer. Look at her face," Fergus requested.

Sam squinted. "Yes, yes, I think it is. Her eyes. Those are my mother's eyes. Why is my mother visible in this bowl? What does that mean?"

"I think I might know. Sylvia formed a connection when she had the vision of your mother. That connection is still going, and your mother is appearing in the bowl. I have an idea," announced Fergus. If the connection was still strong, Sam may be able to get a message to the woman. "Sam, I need you to hold your hands over the bowl."

Sam cupped his hands and placed them over the bowl. "Now what?"

"Don't touch the water but I want you to think hard, really hard. In your mind, let your mother know you're here," instructed Fergus.

"I don't know how to do that," said Sam, discouraged.

"Of course you do. Focus. Picture her in your mind. Tell her what you would say to her as if she was standing right in front of you," Fergus said with frustration. How could he make Sam understand?

Sam closed his eyes, wrinkled his forehead and grimaced. "It's not working."

"Relax. You're trying too hard. Take a deep breath and think of your mother," Fergus said calmly.

"Alright. I think I can do that." Sam closed his eyes and took a deep breath, then exhaled. "I see her. I see her."

"Good, good. Now think in your head the words you want to say to her." Fergus continued gazing into the bowl.

"I'm doing it. I'm telling her I miss her and that I want to be with her again," said Sam with excitement.

"Yes. Yes." Fergus saw the woman in the bowl look up as though she was hearing something.

"Sammy? Sammy?" Fergus heard the thoughts of the woman.

"Sam, she hears you. Keep thinking your thoughts." Fergus leaned closer to the bowl.

"Mama. It's me, Sammy. I'm in the forest. I'm close to you. Don't be afraid." Sam sent more thoughts.

"Fergus, I can feel her. She feels me. I can sense her." Sam was delighted.

"Yes, she can." Fergus heard the woman's thoughts again. "Sammy, I hear you. Where are you? Do not come here. It is not safe." The woman's fear was intense.

Fergus repeated the thoughts to Sam. "Tell her you are safe and that we are trying to find a way to rescue her."

Sam sent the thoughts and Fergus could see a look of relief on the woman's face as it rippled in water in the bowl. "She knows. She knows. Sam, you did it."

"She knows you're alive, Sam. And you now know the woman is your mother. Now we need to work out a plan to rescue her and get you all safely home. No small deed." Fergus had no idea of what to do now. "I don't think Phillip can help us with this." Suddenly, Fergus had an idea. He rushed off to where Sylvia kept her potions. "She must have it here, somewhere. I know it." He gazed over all the things stored on the shelves. "Here it is. I knew she would have it." Fergus grabbed a jar that had been sealed with a cork and wax. He took it back into the sitting room.

"What do you have?" Annie asked.

"It's something I had heard of, a mushroom," Fergus remarked.

"What kind of mushroom?" Sam asked.

"It's called the wish mushroom and it is shaped like a heart. It has special powers," Fergus replied.

Sam was now curious. "What does it do?"

"I believe it can help you to help someone else, as long as you have great love with a pure and loving heart. Wait, I have an idea." Fergus went to the kitchen and grabbed something to write with. "I need paper, something to write on."

Annie jumped up and went searching for paper. "Here. Here's some paper." She handed it to Fergus.

Fergus grabbed the pen in between his feathers, scribbling and drawing. There were lines and circles, trees and walls. "Yes, hmmm. Yes, this could work," Fergus mumbled as he drew. "There. We will try this."

"What? What will we try?" Sam asked anxiously.

"In order for you to safely get to the castle, you need to fly. And for the Black Thatcher to not see you, what needs to happen? It's simple," Fergus remarked.

Annie asked, "What is simple?"

"We have to make it so you can fly and for you to be invisible." Fergus smiled.

CHAPTER SEVENTEEN

It was cold in the castle. The Black Thatcher hurled more logs into the massive stone fireplace. His ornately carved oak throne sat directly in front of the bouncing flames. "Bring me more logs." The Black Thatcher shouted to a gnarled troll-like figure who had been standing guard.

"Yes master," grumbled the creature in reply. It shuffled as it walked away, hunched over with its hands almost reaching the ground.

"Fetch me the woman," the black-cloaked master barked at another guard, one even more ugly than the former. "And make sure she is attired in something festive." He looked in the mirror, admiring his chiseled chin and his pitch-black hair cascading over his broad shoulders. His piercing green eyes were mesmerizing, so he thought. Any woman would be lucky to have him.

The hideous guard could be heard shuffling down the dark damp hall, his long claws scratching the stone floor.

Rivulets of water dripped down the cold walls and bits of moss could be seen growing in the crevices. "Should've kept more creatures around. The castle is looking a bit unkempt," the Black Thatcher mumbled to himself. "But tonight, I will dine with the lovely lady. We will eat the sweetest fruits and drink the finest berry wine. I'm sure Martha is used to the taste." The sinister master laughed as he thought of how many brambled forest beings had been squeezed into the latest batch of wine. "One day, I will convince her to be my Queen. We will rule together."

§ § §

Martha heard the guard as he approached the cold, damp cell. She pulled her shawl tighter around her. She was still shaking from the news that her son was alive, her darling Sammy. Usually, the guard only came to bring her meals or to take her to see the cruel King. She knew he wasn't really a King and that the real King was gone. Often the other prisoners could be heard talking in their cells. They shared enough so that Martha knew how things were before. She knew she had to bow down to the Black Thatcher, or he would have her killed. A bulky, moldy-smelling, hairy creature unlocked the door to Martha's cell.

"You must come. You are to wear something festive," the guard growled.

Martha cringed. This meant that the King wanted to be entertained. She slowly got up from her wooden chair and walked to the wardrobe. The Black Thatcher had filled it with the finest garb - bright silks, warm woolens, and even some brocades from far, far away, he had told her. She preferred her own woven clothing that reminded her of home. She had made some simpler dresses out of the fancy ones. She pulled the threads and rewove it into something more familiar. It helped pass the time and allowed her to remember happier days.

"I will be right there," she shouted to the guard as she slipped behind a screen to change into a red silk dress. She knew the wicked king loved the red dress. Perhaps he would let her go free if she could only please him enough." She grimaced at the thought of the horrible man touching her. "Sammy must not come here. The evil one will surely have him killed." Martha tried imagining her son. It had been so many years, yet his face was still etched in her mind. How could he be alive? Was he in some sort of purgatory, a place between heaven and hell? How is it that Sammy could speak to her?

"Hurry. We must not keep the master waiting," the guard snarled.

"I'm ready." Martha grabbed her shawl and followed the guard out of the room that had been her home for longer than she realized. She had lost track. There was no mirror and no calendar. She had no way to know what day or year it was. She counted herself lucky that her skin still felt young and unwrinkled and she could see that her long hair was still a vibrant chestnut color. There wasn't a gray hair in sight. "He must find me attractive or he wouldn't want my company," she thought. "What if that's the only reason I'm still alive?"

The duo walked down the torch-lit halls until they came to the main hall. She could see reflections from the fireplace bouncing off the walls. "At least it'll be warm," she thought.

"Ah, there you are my lovely. Please, come in. Let me take your hand." The Black Thatcher bowed as he gently kissed Martha's hand. "I hope you are well. Tonight, we dine and then we dance." The king led the woman to a seat at the table. "Bring the first course." He clapped his hands.

Servants, green elf-like creatures, appeared from the shadows bringing an assortment of bread, cheese, and fruit. "Splendid." The black-cloaked man smiled as he gazed over the full table.

Martha placed a slice of cheese and a piece of bread on her plate. She added a few grapes. "Delicious."

"Is that all you have to say? This is the finest food in the land," the self-appointed King's voice announced with pride.

"Yes, my lord. It is perhaps the tastiest food I have ever had." Martha knew to say what would make this monster happy. Any acts of defiance always resulted in being denied food later in her cell.

"Wine. Where is the wine?" the Black Thatcher shouted to a servant.

"Here your Grace." A shaking elf poured the purple juice into two glasses, the bottle clanking on the glass rim.

"More. More. I want these glasses full." The fake King waited for the servant to fill the glasses then watched as the elf bowed, and slowly backed away.

"Here my sweet maiden. Drink this fine wine." The wicked man pushed a glass towards Martha.

"I really am not thirsty. Perhaps later." The woman politely refused, knowing the wine must be bewitched in some way.

"You will drink this wine, now," the evil lord said sternly.

Martha picked up the glass and took a sip, her face puckering at the bitter taste.

"More. You will drink more," the Black Thatcher ordered in a loud booming voice.

The woman continued to drink until the glass was empty. "My head is spinning. I feel ill."

"You need more food." Again, the Black Thatcher clapped his hands and shouted at the servants. "Food. Bring us more food."

Venison on platters and huge bowls of turnips were placed on the table. The King piled his platter high, stuffing bite after bite into his mouth. "Why aren't you eating? I order you to eat." The gluttonous man shoved a plate closer to the ill woman.

"I am not hungry, your Grace. Really, I do not feel well at all. I believe I drank too much wine." Martha rubbed her stomach and then her head. "Please, might I go back to my room and lie down?"

"Guards. Take the woman back to her room." The Black Thatcher's face showed disappointment.

"Thank you. I am sure I will feel better once I can rest. The food was generous and delicious. Perhaps we can dine together another day." Martha curtsied as she backed away from the table. She leaned heavily on a guard as he brought her back to her room.

Martha heard the clank as the guard locked the door behind her. She collapsed on the bed, her head spinning from the horrible wine. Every time the King asked for her, he would make her drink the terrible juice. It always tasted bitter and her head would spin. Her stomach would wretch for hours afterward. She knew there had to be some sort of black magic attached to the vile liquid. If only he would give her tea instead of that awful wine. Martha remembered the times when she lived in Willow Glen. She would prepare tea and biscuits for Sammy and they would sit at the table and laugh and laugh. Oh, how she missed him. Knowing he might be nearby, brought her some comfort, although she felt maybe it was a dream. So many thoughts crossed her mind. "How could he be here? Why isn't he in heaven? He couldn't possibly be alive after all this time."

"Oh, Sammy. My life ended the day we were separated," Martha cried into her pillow. She remembered the day she fell through time, never to return to the life she had before that horrible day. It began with a simple visit to the church. She remembered the deep grief she had felt because Sammy had died. She wanted to light candles at the church but there weren't any. She knew the church storage room had them so she went there to get candles. She saw the trunk and thought perhaps they were stored there. As she leaned in, she fell. She remembered herself falling, falling, to a place she'd never seen. She had hit her head and couldn't remember anything for many years. Someone cared for her at first but she had a hard time remembering who it was. The Black Thatcher captured her and she'd been imprisoned ever since. Once her memory returned, she thought of Sammy and the life she'd had before. Years and years went by, yet she never aged. She couldn't explain it. Sometimes she wanted to die, to go to heaven and be away from the horrible prison cell.

Martha grabbed a bucket and heaved into the wooden pail. It happened every time she drank the vile juice. With the rain beating against the castle walls, Martha fell asleep on the rickety bed, her body shaking from the cold.

§§§

The Black Thatcher hurled a plate across the room. "How dare she not want to dine with me. I give her the best food and the finest wine. Maybe I should tell her that the juice is what is keeping her alive, that it is how she maintains her beauty. She would thank me for sure." He hurled a turkey leg at a guard. "Clean this up," he shouted to the servants. He wanted this woman, his future Queen, to love him but what did he have to offer her? If he released her, she would run away. He needed to make sure she would never leave, or he would only have the guards as companions. So much could go wrong. If he lost the brambles, he would lose access to the bramble juice. He needed the brambles to stay alive. It had been many years since he bewitched the forest. Time had taken a toll on the woodland creatures and all who had ventured above ground, had been brambled. He was running out of animals to trap and the fairies, pixies, and trolls had figured out how to avoid the brambles. Thankfully he had many bottles stored of the bramble juice, the elixir of immortality. There was another plan he had carefully thought out, but he would need to capture Sylvia, that horrible woman in the forest who had defied him.

"Sylvia, oh yes Sylvia. And how does it feel to be trapped in the shadows for the rest of eternity?" The King laughed a sinister sound as he thought of the curse he placed on the woman in the forest. "I will come to see you soon. I know you have magic I can force out of you."

CHAPTER EIGHTEEN

Fergus drew sketches and wrote symbols on a piece of paper. He knew the children were counting on him. "This must work."

"Is that the plan? Is that how we are going to rescue my mother?" Sam leaned closer to see.

"Sam, I can't see. Move over." Annie pushed the boy to the side.

"Children, there is nothing you need to see. I need you to get your knapsacks and don't forget those vials," Fergus instructed.

"Mine is still in my pocket," Annie commented.

"So is mine. What are they for?" Sam asked.

"You will know when you need to know. For now, I need you to gather all your things as we won't be coming back here." Fergus walked around the cabin, blowing out candles and latching windows. "I want to make sure we leave nothing behind of a magical nature." He scooped a shelf full of bottles and jars into a burlap sack then walked through the cabin checking every cupboard and closet. "We don't want any of this to fall into the hands of the Black Thatcher."

The children found their belongings and used the buckets for the last time. "Fergus, do you think Sylvia would mind if I took her knitting? I would like my mother to have it. Perhaps she could finish knitting Sylvia's socks." Sam's voice wavered a little, as emotions set in.

"Splendid idea. I'm sure Sylvia would like that." Fergus watched Sam stuff the yarn and needles into his knapsack. "Come here, children. It's time to get ready to fly." Fergus opened the jar of wish mushrooms.

"Those sure don't look like they're going to taste very good." Annie made a face. "I've never seen pink mushrooms before."

"They don't smell very good either." Sam pinched his nose shut.

"I need you to both listen to me. The only way these mushrooms will work is for there to be great love. How can the magic work if you're complaining about how bad something tastes and smells?" Fergus lectured.

"You're right. Annie, this will help us save my mother and get us home. You want that, right?" Sam looked into his friend's eyes. "I need you to do this for me, and for us. Please?"

"Of course I want this. I want to go home too. And if you can be with your mother again, oh Sam, that would make me so happy." The young girl gave Sam a big hug.

"That's better. Here. You need a spoonful. Don't chew it. Swallow it down. A swig of moss tea might help." Fergus doled out the servings and had a cup of tea ready, just in case. He had only tasted wish mushrooms once and from his recollection, they tasted awful.

Sam and Annie chugged down the mushrooms and each took a big gulp of tea. "I don't feel anything," Sam said.

"Me neither." Annie closed her eyes. "Although my tongue feels funny. Wait. Now my ears feel funny."

"Mine too." Sam flailed his arms. "Look, my arms have feathers." Sam looked down at the black feathers punching through the sleeves of his coat.

"I have feathers too." Annie's arms were now covered in white feathers. "And look. Even my behind has feathers."

Fergus laughed. "I knew this was to help you fly but I didn't think you'd be turning into birds. This will be an adventure." The big crow pushed the children from the cottage and closed the door. Flying came natural to him but telling someone how to fly was complicated. "Take three big hops and leap up. Flap your arms and the feathers will do the rest." Fergus watched as Sam and Annie hopped, ran, then soared into the air. He breathed a sigh of relief.

"Look. I'm flying," Annie shouted to Sam.

"Me too." Sam went higher and higher until he was above the tallest of the trees.

"Wait for me." Fergus was right behind them as the trio headed for the castle of the Black Thatcher.

Soaring over the trees, Fergus and the children flew closer and closer to the castle. "Stay close behind me. I know a good place to land where we won't be seen," shouted Fergus to the two human birds, hoping that they wouldn't lose their feathers midflight. "There. Behind that wall." The large crow landed first and waited as Annie and Sam tumbled in a heap of feathers, to his side.

"You didn't tell us how to land," Sam grumbled as he tucked in his wings and shook off the bad landing.

"Ouch. That hurt." Annie rubbed her head. "Now what? We can't go walking around looking like this."

"No. Of course not. The flying spell should be wearing off soon. Another gulp of mushrooms and we can move on to the next part of the plan." Fergus pulled out the jar of mushrooms and passed it around. He even kept some mushrooms for himself. "We will wait here and rest. I'm sure you are a bit tired from flying."

"My arms feel like they're going to fall off," Sam complained.

"Flying sure isn't easy."

"My feathers are starting to go away. Look." Annie pointed at a swirling column of white feathers which disappeared before her eyes.

"Mine too," said Sam.

"Hopefully I will get to keep mine," said Fergus, laughing softly. He tried to picture himself as a plucked crow. "We need to keep our voices down. There are guards everywhere." Fergus peered over the wall and noticed a guard near a large door. He looked like one of the creatures often spotted in the forest. "Swallow down your mushrooms now. The next part of the plan is to make ourselves invisible so we can enter the castle without being seen. It's important to focus on being invisible. Get the thoughts strong in your minds before you swallow. I can't tell you how the next part of this spell will feel. Don't make any noise," instructed Fergus.

"Ew. That tasted worse than the first time." Sam's face twisted in disgust.

"It's not so bad." Annie held her nose this time.

Fergus tilted back his beak and tossed in a few pieces of mushroom. The spell worked quickly and all three were soon totally invisible to everyone but themselves. "Shhh. We will need to walk quietly and no talking. Just because we can't be seen doesn't mean we still can't be heard. I will lead the way. Make sure to not make a sound." Fergus was concerned that the plan he had wasn't very well thought out. What if they were spotted? What if the children were captured? It would be all his fault. He had to make sure that everything worked. "Tiptoe," Fergus whispered. "Sound echoes in the castle."

They moved slowly towards the large wooden door where a guard seemed to be deep in thought. Fergus had another of Sylvia's jars that he had grabbed before leaving the cottage. He thought it might come in handy. He pulled it from his bag and pulled the cork, pouring a small bit of dust onto his wingtip. "Poof." Fergus blew a handful of sleep sprinkle into the guard's face. The guard crumpled to the ground. "That was easy," Fergus whispered. "Here, help me with the door." They all pulled, and the door creaked open.

"Do you know which way to go?" Sam asked.

"Let's try this way." Fergus led the children down a narrow hallway. "Over there. Look, another guard." Fergus again blew some sleep dust and the hallway guard crumpled to the cold stone floor. "This is much easier than I thought it'd be."

"Over there. There is light coming from under that door." Annie pointed to a wooden door that had a streak of light shining below it. "Do you think that's where Sam's mother is?" Annie spoke as softly as she could.

"We will have to take a chance." Fergus unlatched the bolt and pulled with all his might. The door was too heavy. "I need your help. Let's pull together." The trio pulled and pulled until finally, the door swung open. The hinges creaked and the trio stopped in their tracks.

"Do you think anyone heard that?" Sam sounded worried.

"There's no time to wait and see. Quick, inside." Fergus pushed Annie and Sam into the room. A woman was sound asleep on a bed, a candle burning on the table beside her.

Sam walked slowly towards the sleeping figure. "I'm scared. What if it's not her and this was all for nothing?"

"Oh Sam. There's no reason for you to be worried," Annie said.

The spell was still working so even if the woman woke up, she would not be able to see the three standing near her the bed. "We don't want to scare her. Maybe we should wait until we can be seen before we wake her up?" Fergus spoke in hushed tones.

Sam moved closer and looked at the face of the woman on the bed. "She looks so young. How is that possible?"

Fergus suspected that the Black Thatcher had bewitched the woman. "Sam, there are ways that the Black Thatcher keeps himself alive. It's in the bramble juice. At least that's what Ornoth told me. Maybe your mother had to drink the juice? That would keep her young."

"That's what Annie said, too. But maybe it's an enchantment or something. Maybe she didn't have to drink the elixir?" Sam sounded hopeful.

Sam's form became visible. "I think the spell is wearing off," Sam whispered.

Fergus looked at the children and saw their shapes become clearer. "We must move fast. Sam, I am not sure how your mother would react to a talking crow, so you better be the one to wake her up." Fergus moved to a corner of the room where he wouldn't be noticed right away.

Sam rested his hand on the woman's face. "Mama. It's me. Sammy." The woman stirred, then pulled the blanket tighter.

"Mama, please. Wake up. It's me, Sam. We need to hurry," said Sam with urgency.

"Sam?" The woman opened her eyes. "Sammy! Sammy!" She reached for the boy and pulled him towards her. Her eyes filled with tears. "You're here. How can this be? You died. How can you be here?" Her eyes grew large, and then full of fear. She pushed the boy away, so hard he fell to the ground. "You're a demon, sent to trick me. This is an evil spell that the Black Thatcher has done. Go away."

"No Mama. No. It's really me. I'm really here." Sam stood up and moved close to the bed. "Annie, tell her. Tell her I'm not a demon."

"Mrs. Sullivan. I'm Annie, Sam's friend. He's telling the truth. He has been looking for you for a long time." Annie took the woman's hand. "We have traveled back in time, through a trunk, and Sam is alive again. He had been unable to cross to heaven. He was waiting for you and something went wrong," Annie explained.

"A trunk? You traveled in a trunk?" Martha's surprised face finally showed belief.

"The fairies never came to get him," Annie remarked.

The woman appeared confused. "Fairies. What fairies?"

"The ones that help people cross over, of course. They never came. Sam has been living in the forest near Willow Glen for over a hundred years," Annie replied.

The woman's hand flew to her mouth. Her face showed horror. "You mean Sam has been dead all this time, unable to get to heaven?"

"Yes Mama. I thought you would come for me. I waited and waited." Tears ran down the boy's face.

"But I can feel you. You're alive now. How can that be?" Sam's mother was confused. "You're not a demon?"

"No Mama. I am still a boy and I am very much alive." Sam held his mother's hand. "See? You can touch me." He moved her hand to his heart. "Feel my heart. Listen. It's beating."

"It is you. Oh Sammy. How did you ever find me here?" Martha still had so many questions.

"We found a trunk at the church and we fell into it and it spun and tumbled and somehow landed in a forest, this forest," explained Sam. "When I climbed out of the trunk, my head was bleeding. I was breathing and my heart was beating, and I discovered I was alive again." The words poured out.

"The church? That's where I was too," said the woman, recalling her memory. "A trunk, yes. I was spinning, feeling like I was going to faint. Before I knew it, I had landed in this forest. I have seen many strange things here."

"Such as myself?" Fergus walked out of the shadows.

The woman gasped. "Wha... what, who are you?"

"I'm Fergus. I'm a friend of Annie and Sam's. Please don't be afraid. We are here to rescue you from the Black Thatcher."

"I'm not afraid. Believe me, I have seen all kinds of creatures at this castle. They usually aren't around long though, except for the trolls, the King's guards. The moldy ones. Sometimes their stench is more than I can bear." Martha grimaced.

"We weren't sure you were really Sam's mother," Fergus spoke up.

"My name is Martha, Martha Sullivan. Thank you so much for helping bring Sam to me. Yes, I am indeed his mother."

"You mentioned King. The Black Thatcher is calling himself King now?" Fergus sounded annoyed.

"Yes, although I have heard stories that he isn't really a King at all," Martha stated.

"He is not the rightful King. He is an imposter, an evil sorcerer. I am sorry but you have been bewitched, kept here for many years by someone wicked and dangerous." Fergus disliked telling the woman these things.

"How am I bewitched?" Martha seemed confused.

"Haven't you wondered how you have stayed so young? Why you have lived for years and years with no signs of aging?" Fergus asked.

"Young? What do you mean? I am very old. I know I have been here for many years," the woman replied.

"Mama, Fergus is right. It has been over a hundred years since I died. You have been here that long. How are you still alive?" Sam asked.

Martha looked down at her hands. She felt her hair. Bursting into tears she cried out, "If I am cursed, how can I ever leave? If I do, won't I die?"

Sam wrapped his arms around his mother. "No matter what happens, we will be together now. Please don't cry."

CHAPTER NINETEEN

"Guards. Get my carriage ready. I want to take a trip into the forest," shouted the Black Thatcher as he barked orders to his creatures. He strode boldly through the large castle room, his black cloak swirling behind him. The day was overcast and drizzly. The Black Thatcher thought perhaps Sylvia would be out in the forest picking her special flowers and herbs, since the sun was hidden behind the dark clouds.

"Take me through the back glen. I want to sneak up on that old witch. She is probably harvesting out in the meadow. I know exactly where it is," the evil man snarled.

"Yes, my lord," the driver replied.

The road was muddy and bumpy, and the Black Thatcher held tightly to the polished handles inside his elegant carriage. He hadn't been into the forest in months. It was very quiet, other than the sound of the rattling wheels over the bumpy road that traversed through the bewitched forest. "Stop. Stop here," the Black Thatcher ordered from the window. One of his guards helped him climb down from the carriage.

"Your Grace, would you like me to accompany you?" the guard asked.

"No. Stay here. I won't be long." The evil one gazed out on the meadow where he knew Sylvia collected herbs. The woman was nowhere in sight. "Maybe she's already come and gone?" he thought. He searched for footprints in the grass but nothing had been disturbed. The plants showed no signs of having been picked recently. "She's not here," the Black Thatcher shouted in anger, as he kicked the dirt.

The guard helped the Black Thatcher into the carriage and shut the door. "Shall we go back to the castle?" the guard asked.

"No. Tell the driver I want to go to Sylvia's cabin." Sinister thoughts filled the dark lord's head. "That witch will be sorry she was ever born," he muttered out loud.

The moss-covered cottage was nestled back in the shadows, not even visible from the road. The Black Thatcher knew exactly how to find it, the spell still fresh in his mind that he had placed on the elderly woman. "She will be surprised to see me," he laughed. The horses stopped in front of the thatched home and one of the guards quickly appeared to open the carriage door. The Black Thatcher stepped down, then strode quickly up to the front door and thrust it open. "Sylvia, you won't be able to hide from me." His wicked laugh broke through the stillness.

"Your Grace, your sword," the troll-faced guard tossed the silver-bladed weapon to his master.

Going room to room, the cloaked man searched for the medicine woman, flailing his sword through the air. He knew she had to be here somewhere but there were no signs of her. Even the tea kettle was cold. "Where are you? Have you made yourself invisible? You can't escape me. I will find you," his voice booming through the cottage. He looked outside the cabin and was surprised to find no footprints.

"Guard. Throw me a satchel," the angry lord shouted to the foul-smelling creature, one of many creatures he had bewitched. There were no humans around so finding trolls, elves and dwarves to serve him was the best he could do. The King caught the burlap bag that his guard had thrown. "I should get her potions while I'm here." The Black Thatcher went into each room looking for the pouches and vials he knew Sylvia stored on her shelves. "That's odd. Where are all the potions? There aren't even any herbs hanging in the kitchen. Sylvia? What have you done?" The Black Thatcher stomped through Sylvia's cabin. He realized the woman had gone and taken her potions with her. He wasn't sure how this was possible. His spell was unbreakable.

With fury in his eyes, the angry man picked up a table and hurled it across the room. He took the axe from the porch and broke everything he could find. He slashed open Sylvia's mattress and watched feathers fill the air. "You can't escape me. If you are hiding in the forest, you will have no cabin to return to." The Black Thatcher stormed out of the cabin and climbed into the carriage. "Burn it. Burn it to the ground," the wicked one ordered.

One of the guards lit a torch and threw it into the cabin.

Laughing hysterically the evil one shouted, "You should know better than to hide from me." Smoke billowed through the trees as flames licked through the door and windows of the cabin. Soon all that was left was a pile of ash, the chimney all that remained.

CHAPTER TWENTY

"Do you hear that?" Annie asked.

"What?" Fergus looked up. His eyesight was better than his hearing.

"I hear footsteps. Listen." Annie walked towards the cell door. "I can feel the floor shaking. The sound is getting closer.

Fergus approached the door but before he could identify the sound, the door burst open.

"What have we here?" A loud voice boomed as the Black Thatcher stormed into the small room. "Ahh. Two humans and a crow, a very large crow. You should fill many bottles of elixir. Guards. Take them to the dungeon and prepare them for brambling."

"No. No. You can't take us. This is my mother. Why are you keeping her here? Please let me stay with her," Sam pleaded.

"Your mother? I see. She never mentioned she had a child. Guards, take them," the evil lord yelled.

"No, my lord. Please don't take them. Please. I will do whatever you want. Don't take my son and his friends." The woman grabbed the King's robes, begging him to spare the trio who had come to rescue her.

"Mamaaaa... Don't forget me," Sam cried out as the moldy guards pulled him away.

"You are a wicked, wicked man," Annie shouted at the Black Thatcher, her arms flailing as she resisted the guard's slimy grasp.

"And you crow. I finally have you where I want you. I have seen you flying over the castle, always out of reach of the brambles. My guess is you had something to do with Sylvia's disappearance."

Fergus glanced at the children and shook his head, attempting to warn them not to say anything. "I know nothing of this," Fergus uttered.

"Sylvia, the medicine woman in the forest. I know you are friends with her. What do you know about her?" The Black Thatcher grabbed Fergus by the throat and shook him until feathers flew.

"Yes, I know Sylvia. I have not seen her in many months." Fergus pretended that he hadn't just lost a close friend.

"She has vanished but I will find her. She won't be able to hide from me for long." The Black Thatcher's anger was evident. "And as for you crow, you have finally run out of luck. Take them all away." The King gestured to the guards.

"You won't get away with this," Fergus shouted, his wings forced behind him as the guards dragged him down the hallway. He attempted to get closer to the children but to no avail.

"Annie, stay close to me. We will get through this. Hold onto my hand." Sam reached for Annie and pulled her closer. "Do what the guard says."

The repugnant guard threw the three into a cell and locked the metal door. "At least we are together," said Fergus with relief. They could still talk to each other and make a plan.

"What do we do now Fergus?" Sam asked the stooped over bird. "We are going to be brambled. We won't be able to rescue my mother or get home." The young boy could not contain his tears.

Annie sobbed, "I miss my parents. I miss Sadie. I want to go home."

"Please try not to worry. I have an idea." Fergus plucked some feathers from his chest. "Quick, get out your vials, the ones Ornoth gave you."

Sam reached in his pocket and pulled out a vial. "Here's mine."

Annie reached for her vial and removed it from her pocket. "I had forgotten about this."

"Open your vials and put in one of these." Fergus handed each of the children one of his feathers. "I want you to place a drop of the potion on your forehead."

"What will this do?" Sam asked as he dabbed his forehead with the oil.

"There is no time to explain. Do as I say." Fergus stepped back. The children started to fade. "It's working." Fergus had little time.

"Fergus, I can't see you. Fergus, I'm ..." Sam's voice sounded in the distance.

The large crow hoped that his plan could protect the children. He now had to wait.

CHAPTER TWENTY-ONE

Sam felt himself being tossed around in a whirling tunnel. He noticed the ground looming towards him and he tumbled and rolled until finally coming to a stop. He reached for his head, hoping to stop the throbbing pain. "Where am I?" Sam looked around and he saw something familiar. He had landed in front of Ornoth's cabin.

"Thank goodness. We thought we'd lost you." Ornoth lumbered out of the cabin, grabbed Sam's arm, and went quickly back inside.

Sam saw Annie seated at the table. "Sam. I was so worried you got lost in the tunnel."

"Tunnel? What tunnel?" Sam asked.

"That thing we traveled through. It brought us here, to Ornoth's house. We are safe." Annie sipped some moss tea. "I've been here for hours. You must've been trapped in the spiral."

"But it was so quick. What do you mean you've been here for hours?" Sam questioned. None of this made any sense. Moments ago, they had been at the castle.

"Annie arrived yesterday. She told me all about the Black Thatcher and your mother and the guards. You are very lucky that Fergus was able to activate your homing potion." Ornoth brought Sam some moss tea. "Here. This will help stop the spinning. It lasts for a bit after going through the tunnel."

"Fergus. What about Fergus? He's not here? What if the Black Thatcher brambles him?" Sam shouted. Now he was worried about his crow friend. Sam knew The Black Thatcher would not let the bird escape.

"We can't worry about Fergus now. He will have to figure out how to break free. He won't leave without your mother, I'm sure of it," said Ornoth with confidence.

"How will he do that?" Sam asked. He suddenly remembered his mother, how she was trapped in that awful cell.

"Fergus knows many things. He was taught by Sylvia of the Shadows. She knows much about magic," Ornoth said proudly.

"Sylvia was so kind to us. If it wasn't for her, we never would've known Sam's mother was being held in the castle." Annie's eyes welled up.

"Sylvia is extra special. I can't wait to see her again," Ornoth replied.

"But you can't." Sam thought about the fairies taking Sylvia away. He looked at Ornoth. "You don't know, do you? Annie, why didn't you tell him?"

"I was so worried about you, I forgot." Annie covered her face with her hands to hide her tears.

"Don't know what? And why can't I see her? She is a good friend," Ornoth said.

"Ornoth. The most horrible thing happened. She was helping us, and we were asleep and when she went to bed, she forgot to cover the window and she… she died. The fairies came for her." Sam bowed his head, remembering the sight of Sylvia being turned into fairy dust.

"Oh, no. That is terrible news," said Ornoth, his voice shaking with sadness. A tear slid down his cheek. "Did she tell you about the curse? The one the Black Thatcher placed on her?"

"Somewhat. Fergus told us the rest. We had been sleeping and we found her dead in her bed. Thank goodness Fergus showed up when he did," said Sam. "He said it was the sunlight through the window that killed her. She forgot to close the curtain."

Annie continued the story. "Then Fergus summoned the fairies. They took her to the realm in between blinks."

"It is indeed unfortunate that Sylvia couldn't help you," Ornoth stated. "She would've known what to do."

"Oh, but she did. She summoned Fergus," announced Sam. "He saved us. They both saved us."

"Sylvia was knitting socks. My mother used to knit socks. Sam took the knitting. He was going to give it to his mother. But now he can't." Annie's sad eyes glanced at Sam.

Ornoth grew quiet. He stood up and then paced back and forth, his hands clasped behind him. "What to do, what to do..." He mumbled. "My friend Sylvia is gone. This is indeed sad news. My other friend Fergus is locked in the dungeon at the castle. The Black Thatcher must be stopped."

"What do we do now?" Sam asked.

"We must get help to Fergus, first and foremost," Ornoth said. "Was there anything he said, anything that can help us know what to do?"

"No. He plucked feathers from his chest and placed in the vials you gave us. Before we even had a chance to say good-bye, we were whisked away." Sam pulled out his vial.

"His feathers. Yes. That's it." Ornoth went into the back room where Fergus perched to sleep. "Here. Here is one that will work." Ornoth returned with two small wisps of black feathers. "Hand me your vials." Ornoth watched as the children placed their vials in his hand. "We can go in reverse. This potion has many abilities." Ornoth removed the corks and added the feathers.

"You mean you want us to go back to the castle? If we do, we will be brambled for sure," Annie said.

"Not you. Me," Ornoth said. "You stay here. I will go get Fergus."

"But what about my mother? Who will rescue her?" Sam said with worry. All these attempts seemed in vain.

143

"Ah yes, your mother. Let me ponder this. If we rescue her, the Black Thatcher may have a spell placed on her that could result in her death, just like Sylvia. I must think this through." The troll recorked the vials and placed the feathers in his pocket. "Perhaps the reverse spell won't work as I'd thought." Ornoth again paced, his hands clasped behind his back.

Annie patted a spot on the bench beside her. "Sam, come sit here with me. Let's have some tea. Ornoth needs time to figure this out."

"But I want to help. She's my mother. I should be the one who rescues her." Sam was frustrated. Nothing seemed to be working. He worried that Ornoth would not be able to do this all alone, or even worse, that he wouldn't come up with a plan at all.

Annie reasoned with the boy. "You need to relax, Sam. Worrying will get us nowhere. And remember, this is about magic. You don't know magic. Ornoth does." Annie handed Sam a biscuit.

"I could learn. I need to use the potion, like Ornoth said." Sam swallowed the biscuit and poured a cup of tea, although he really wasn't hungry. Time was wasting. Why couldn't they go now?

CHAPTER TWENTY-TWO

"Remove your hands from me, you wretched creature," Fergus shouted at the guard who smelled like rotten fish. "I can walk on my own. I do not need your help."

The slimy guard searched the room. "Where are the children?" He barked.

"What children? Only I am here. Do you see any children?" Fergus ruffled his feathers.

"What have you done with them?" The guard swung his grotesque arms around. "They are here. You have hidden them."

"Feel free to look all you want. There are no children here." Fergus sat down and waited, his wings stretched casually behind his head.

"Come. You must go to the master." The ugly creature poked Fergus with the handle of his axe. "Go."

"You don't need to do that." Fergus felt the sting from the stick. "I will go. Stop poking me."

The creature and the crow walked down the hall. Fergus could see the fireplace reflection bouncing on the wall. They were getting close to the great room.

"Master. Here is your prisoner. The children have escaped." The guard bowed to the black cloaked man who was sitting at his feast table.

"What? How can that be? You took them all to the dungeon." The Black Thatcher jumped up. "It is you. You helped them escape." He turned to Fergus.

"I don't know what you mean. I was alone in the cell. The guard must've lost them on the way there," explained Fergus.

"You are lying," the evil one shouted.

"If I had helped them escape, wouldn't I have gone with them?" Fergus replied.

The Black Thatcher appeared furious. He walked back and forth, his cloak billowing behind him. "Find those children or you will be brambled," the master shouted at the guard.

"Yes, my lord. I will get the others and begin the search." The guard bent down with his fist clenched to his chest. "In service, my lord."

Fergus waited for the guard to leave. "What are your plans for me?"

"Silence bird or I might have my servants prepare crow stew for supper." The evil one sat down in his chair, his long black hair billowing down his back.

Fergus knew it would be best to remain silent. Still, he needed to find out as much as he could about the castle, the guards, and what the Black Thatcher was thinking. "You have a fine castle here. I remember it when someone else was the King."

The Black Thatcher turned; his face filled with rage. "I am the King now. The former King is no more."

"Where did he go, might I ask?" Fergus hoped the cloaked man would give him some clues; any information that might help him know what happened to the previous King.

"He was a joke, an embarrassment, dancing around with his stupid little sword. I knew he wasn't fit to be King. I banished him, sent him away. He will never return." The Black Thatcher strutted towards the fireplace. "He must be dead by now," said the dark one, followed by an evil laugh. "And if by some chance he escaped my brambles, he is forever cursed."

"Your brambles are amazing. Never have I seen such fast-moving vines. Good thing I can fly." Fergus was getting closer to the truth. He had to keep the Black Thatcher talking. "I remember once when my friend was wrapped in your brambles. I thought for sure he was a goner."

"He escaped?" asked the King.

"Of course he escaped. He had his best friend with him," Fergus proudly stated.

"And his friend escaped too?" The Black Thatcher sounded concerned. "Nothing escapes my brambles. There must've been magic at work."

"No magic. Just brute strength," Fergus said as he chuckled.

"Who is this friend? Where does he live? Is he in my forest?" the evil lord demanded.

"If I told you that, you'd go search for him. I don't think he'd like that very much," taunted Fergus.

"You must take me to him. If he is in my forest, he must be brambled. And you too. Now that I have you in my grasp, you will make some fine elixir." The master rubbed his hands together.

The clever bird pondered his thoughts. "If I can lead the Black Thatcher to Ornoth, that would buy some time. The children should have arrived by then and would already have told Ornoth what was going on. They would be ready. But Sam's mother; how could she be rescued?" Fergus weighed all the possibilities. There was one thing that kept going through his mind. "The sword. The stupid little sword, as the Black Thatcher had put it. What if…"

"Guard. Tie this bird's wings. I don't want him flying away. And get my carriage ready. We are going hunting," the evil lord barked.

Fergus stood still as the guard wrapped rope around his wings, tying knots after each loop.

"Bring him to the carriage." The Black Thatcher stomped away, his boots pounding on the floor.

The air was cold, and the trees rustled in the wind. Fergus looked towards the castle before being shoved into the shiny black carriage. The Black Thatcher sat opposite him. "On days like this, I am thankful for my feathers. There is a chill in the air."

"Silence. I don't want to hear you talk again," the Black Thatcher shouted at the bird.

Fergus closed his eyes. He had a plan but must not let it be known to the evil cloaked man sitting only an arm's length away. "I sure would love a cup of moss tea." Fergus thought to himself. "Ornoth, I'm on my way."

§§§

"They're coming," Ornoth shouted to the children.

"Who's coming?" Sam asked.

"Fergus and the Black Thatcher. We must get ready." Ornoth hurried the children to a wardrobe in the back room. "I want you to stay in here and do not come out under any circumstances."

"But, what…" Sam stuttered.

"I will only tell you this. Fergus sent me a thought. He has that ability under times of great danger. He is coming here with the Black Thatcher. This is the chance we have been waiting for, but I must know that you are safe," Ornoth explained to Sam and Annie.

"But I'm afraid. The Black Thatcher was going to bramble us. If he knows we are here, he's going to capture us again," Annie said.

"That's what Fergus and I plan on stopping. Please, promise me you will do as I say?" Ornoth pleaded. "Hide in the cabinet. You will be safe there."

"Yes, yes, we will." Sam grabbed Annie's hand and they climbed into the wardrobe.

"I will let you know when it's safe to come out." Ornoth closed the door behind them.

There wasn't much time. Ornoth went to a small trap door hidden beneath the rug in the front room. He grabbed a candle, opened the door and went down the creaky ladder. The space was all dirt with boards that kept the walls in place. Spiders hung in the corners and clods of soil crumbled away from the sides each time Ornoth bumped into them. He held the candle out in front of him looking, searching. "Ah. Here it is." He removed a stone from the wall and reached his arm into the hole behind it. "Yes. It is still here." Ornoth pulled a long sword from the damp soil. "Needs a bit of cleaning up." The troll dusted off what dirt he could feel. He held the sword in one hand and the candle in the other, going slowly up the ladder. "I thought I would never see this day." Ornoth gazed at the bejeweled sword, the sword given to him so many years ago. "It is time."

CHAPTER TWENTY-THREE

The carriage bumped and rocked on its way to Ornoth's cabin. Fergus knew he was taking a risk, hoping that Ornoth had received his thought message. It was something the two of them did, especially when Fergus was out flying looking for food to bring back to the cabin. Fergus would transmit a thought to Ornoth and Ornoth would return a thought, a form of mental communication. "Please Ornoth. Hear me. The Black Thatcher is coming. I told him about you and the cabin. He wants to bramble you, I'm sure. Be ready."

The evil King poked Fergus with his walking stick. "Won't be long now. You and your friend have escaped my brambles long enough. You should fill up many bottles of elixir." The Black Thatcher rubbed his stomach. "I might also add a couple of children, once I find them. They must be hidden in the castle somewhere. There is no way they could've escaped my guards."

Fergus sat back, relieved that Ornoth had thought to give the children the vials of potion before they left for the pixie cave. He must've known something would go wrong. And thankfully, Ornoth had told him how to use the potion. Fergus focused on sending another thought. "Ornoth, I hope the children are safe with you. I used the potion like you said. I needed to stay behind. I wanted to rescue Sam's mother."

"Received. I can hear you loud and clear," Ornoth sent a reply. Fergus jerked, startled to have such a clear message in his head. He looked at the Black Thatcher to see if he suspected anything, but the King was too busy staring out the window, looking for anything alive that he could bramble.

"I have a plan, but you must follow my instructions once you arrive. We do not want to arouse the Black Thatcher's suspicions that I am up to something." Ornoth's thought message was planted firmly in Fergus's head.

"Splendid dear friend. We should be there soon. We are in a carriage and the horses are not as fast as I could fly." Fergus sat back and breathed a deep breath. He was pleased to know that Ornoth had a plan.

"How much further?" the Black Thatcher snapped at the black crow.

"Do you expect me to tell you, knowing you are planning to bramble me?" Fergus asked.

"You don't have much choice. Had we stayed in the castle, you would've already been juice. At least this way, you get to say good-bye to your friend." The evil man cackled a wicked laugh.

"I would think you'd know the forest inside and out," Fergus commented.

"I rarely set foot in the forest. I send my trolls to do that. I much prefer to stay in the castle, dining, and being entertained by the future Queen." The cloaked lord smiled.

"So that's it," Fergus thought to himself. "The Black Thatcher plans on keeping Sam's mother alive, to make her the Queen. No wonder she has been there so long."

"There, up ahead. Turn left at the forked road. That will take you to my friend's cabin," Fergus instructed.

"Very well. Very well indeed. This is much easier than I had anticipated. I thought for sure you would've had some plan up your wing, an ambush by those awful pixies or a group of crows attacking me. I guess you don't have as much power as I thought you did," the Black Thatcher announced as his sinister laugh echoed through the carriage.

The carriage pulled up in front of the cabin and one of the ugly guards opened the door, helping the Black Thatcher to step down.

Fergus was pulled from the carriage, the ropes still binding his wings tightly to his body.

"Uh, that wasn't necessary. I can hop down fine on my own." Fergus shook his feathers. He hoped Ornoth had received his message.

CHAPTER TWENTY-FOUR

The door to the cabin flew open. Ornoth stood on the porch, hunched over, his eyes barely looking up. "Who is there? Who has come?"

"Why you are nothing but an ugly troll. Bow down to me. I order it." The Black Thatcher moved towards Ornoth.

"Who speaks? I cannot see you," Ornoth shouted. "I have no eyesight. You must come closer so I can hear you better."

Fergus seemed to catch on. "Ornoth. It's me, Fergus. I have brought the King."

"My feathered friend. It has been so long. Are you well?" Ornoth continued the charade.

"Indeed, although my wings are tied up. For some reason, the King believes I want to fly away." Fergus laughed.

With that news, Ornoth turned towards the voice, still pretending to be blind. "Your Grace, thank you for bringing Fergus home. I have been missing him. Without him, I am lost." Ornoth turned and walked back into the cabin, his hands feeling for the doorway.

"Guards, grab the troll," the evil lord ordered. He watched as his two smelly guards ran towards Ornoth. The Black Thatcher followed his guards, leaving Fergus tied up and guarded.

Fergus uttered a loud caw and shook himself loose from the ropes. He bounded up the steps and jumped into the cabin, the guard too slow to react.

Ornoth saw Fergus escape but still needed to pretend to be blind. He held tightly to the massive jeweled sword with it pointed at the Black Thatcher.

"Ornoth, let me help you," Fergus whispered.

"Fergus my friend. I am so happy you have returned." Ornoth continued the charade as he swung the sword from side to side, making sure not to make eye contact with the Black Thatcher.

"What do you think you're doing?" the cloaked man shouted.

"Do you not recognize me?" Ornoth asked.

"You? Why would I know you? You're an old troll who somehow managed to escape my brambles. Your time has run out. My guards will take that sword from you." The Black Thatcher looked around for his guards, but they were nowhere to be seen.

"I'm afraid your guards won't be any help to you. I made sure they were sucked into the portal. I had it set up before you arrived." Ornoth smiled, although his eyes were still aimed away from the pretend King.

"What portal? What are you talking about?" The angry man sounded confused.

"I am more than merely a troll. Your curse made me that. I am the true King of the Kingdom. Do you not recognize this sword?" Ornoth lunged towards the Black Thatcher, barely missing him, part of the plan.

"The King? I think not. I am the King," the wicked lord yelled. "Ha. Ha. And how can a blind troll expect to hurt me?" The sound of the Black Thatcher's evil laugh shook through the cabin.

"I knew you'd have a plan, but I didn't know about this. So, the story you told me was about you?" Fergus questioned Ornoth, being careful to avoid the Black Thatcher's grasp.

"Yes, Fergus my friend. I am the true King. The Black Thatcher cursed me and I turned into this troll, but he made one mistake." Ornoth swished the sword through the air.

"Mistake? I don't make mistakes," the evil lord shouted as he lunged but missed the troll.

Ornoth laughed as he explained to the imposter. "You must realize that this sword is bewitched. I had forgotten about it but something changed. I believe it was Sylvia who reminded me who I was. She just sent me a message from the other world," Ornoth explained. "I have hidden it all these years, waiting for the time when I would face you again. Many years ago, Sylvia explained to me the powers of the sword, and the magic it held before you acquired it. She told me that a day would come where I would be able to break your curse and restore the sword to its true power. She was the only one who knew that I was the true King. She cared deeply about the forest that you destroyed, and all the beings you brambled. You also placed a curse on her, preventing her from being in sunlight." Ornoth confronted the Black Thatcher.

"Sylvia? The old woman in the forest? What do you know of her?" the angry man barked. "I had her cottage burned to the ground."

"She was more than an old woman. She was a wise woman, a medicine woman, an enchantress, my friend. Yes, your curse kept her trapped in her home, but she still was able to do magic, more than you realized," said Ornoth, his affection evident. "She helped me remember who I was and how to use the sword."

"How could she send you this message?" the Black Thatcher asked.

"She died as a result of your curse. She was taken by the fairies to the next world," Ornoth explained.

The Black Thatcher showed surprise. "Good riddance, I'd say. I am glad she is dead and now you will be too." The lord lunged at Ornoth a second time, attempting to grab the sword, obviously still believing the troll to be blind.

Ornoth took a step to the side and his attacker stumbled, losing his balance. With not a second to spare, Ornoth swung the sword, slicing it straight through the Black Thatcher's neck, severing the evil man's head in one swing. Blood spurted from the jagged neck and the head fell to the ground, rolling across the floor, and coming to a rest at Fergus's clawed feet. "You have met your match, you evil monster," Ornoth shouted.

Fergus hopped back. Blood splattered everywhere. "Ornoth. You did it. You have killed the Black Thatcher. I never knew. All these years and I never knew."

"I had forgotten, some sort of amnesia. Sylvia only recently reminded me." Ornoth smiled at his crow friend.

"Ornoth, you're, you're…" Fergus stepped back; his eyes huge with disbelief.

"What? Why are you backing away?" a voice called out.

"You're, you're changing," Fergus exclaimed, his eyes on the tall man now standing before him, still holding the bloody sword. "The curse. The curse is broken. But wait… Who is that then?" Fergus looked at the man and then pointed at someone on the floor.

The creature slowly stood up. There, next to the tall man, stood Ornoth. A moan sounded from the hunched-over troll. "What happened?"

"Ornoth! Is that you?" Fergus leaned over the groaning troll.

"I feel funny." The troll shook his head. "Who is that?" Ornoth pointed at the man looming over him.

"Let me explain," the man said. "I hope you will understand, but the Black Thatcher apparently thought by cursing me and placing me in your body, that it would kill me in the process. He didn't realize that Sylvia had placed a protection spell on me many years ago. It enabled me, or the essence of me, to still live inside of you without either of us knowing it. I thought I was you, Ornoth, and you probably didn't notice I was sharing your body with you. I am King Steffan, the true King of this land."

Ornoth stood up, appearing a bit unsteady. "That is preposterous." He shook his hands and feet, still unsteady. "However, I do feel somewhat lighter. You mean you've been living inside me all this time?"

Steffan laughed. "I suppose I did take up a large share of space. Thank you Ornoth for being my host all these years. I know it must've been difficult at times."

"My pleasure, your Grace. Although I didn't know it." The troll bowed before the King.

The King smiled and placed his arms around the troll, squeezing him in a tight hug. "I am indebted to you and you will always be safe within my Kingdom. And from here forward, there is no need to bow. I am merely Steffan, to you and to Fergus. You are my dearest friends, now and always."

Fergus heaved a sigh of relief. "My heart is so full. Steffan and Ornoth. I now have two friends where there once was only one. What a blessing that the curse has been broken."

"Yes, I feel the same." Ornoth pulled the crow close and hugged him to his chest. "Oh Fergus, a better friend I have never had; and now I can also include Steffan."

"Let's look outside and see what has changed," Steffan remarked.

The trio walked outside, Steffan standing tall with his newly formed body, Ornoth walking lightly, and Fergus hopping with excitement.

"Look, the guards are gone and so are the brambles," Fergus shouted with glee.

"It's over, it's over," Steffan yelled out with relief. "Wait. The children. I left the children in the wardrobe." Steffan ran back into the cabin, Fergus behind him. "They're in the bedroom."

Fergus hopped ahead of the true King, threw open the wardrobe doors, and there cowering in each other's arms were Sam and Annie.

"Fergus. Oh Fergus. You're here." Annie threw her arms around the huge crow's neck. "We were so worried about you. Who is that?" Annie looked up at the tall man standing in the doorway.

"This is King Steffan. He killed the Black Thatcher and the curse is over." Fergus motioned the King to come closer.

"What? It has only been a short time that we have been inside this wardrobe. Where is Ornoth? Is he alright?" Sam questioned.

"I am fine." Ornoth walked into the room and stood next to Steffan.

"But how? What happened? Where did this King come from? Are we safe?" Sam was full of questions.

Fergus explained. "Ornoth was, I don't know how to tell you, but… Remember when I told you about the sword and the King that the Black Thatcher cursed?"

"Yes, I remember. It was buried under Ornoth's cabin, this cabin," Sam said. "That's why Ornoth was never harmed.

"Ornoth knew the sword was there and that it was protecting him, but there was something he didn't know," Fergus stated.

"Let me finish the story." Steffan stepped forward. "I am Ornoth. Or, I 'was' Ornoth." The King bent down and faced the children. "The Black Thatcher had cursed me, turned me into a troll, into Ornoth. I met Fergus many years ago and he never knew that Ornoth and I were sharing the same body. I had forgotten that I had been the King, the true King," Steffan explained.

"How is that possible?" Annie asked.

"Many things are possible with magic. Some good. Some bad," the King continued. "I, or I mean, Ornoth, retrieved the sword that was hidden years ago. A few days ago, Sylvia sent me a message from the afterworld. She must've known it was time for me to remember about the sword. She could now see things from the other realm not visible to most of us and realized it was time for the sword to be used. I had to face the Black Thatcher in person for it to work, but I did it. I killed him with the same bewitched sword that he had given me so many years ago," said Steffan continuing his story. "Now that he's dead, the curse is lifted. I am a man again and the brambles are gone. The forest should now be safe."

"That is wonderful news. But Ornoth? How could you be Ornoth?" Sam waited for an explanation.

"The Black Thatcher had cursed me and placed me in Ornoth's body, well my essence, my soul. He probably thought Ornoth would be killed in the process but because Ornoth had a protection spell placed on him by Sylvia, he was able to live even though I was in his body. I imagine it was cozy in there, although I don't remember much." Steffan laughed.

"I am so glad Ornoth is okay," Annie replied. "I wish Sylvia could've protected herself."

Ornoth walked into the room, still shaken at all that had happened. "Is everything alright in here?"

"Ornoth, are you okay?" The children both ran to the troll and wrapped their arms around him.

"I am fine, although my body does feel a bit different. How are the two of you?" Ornoth held the children tight.

"Much better now," Annie replied.

"I think it's time for some moss tea. Would anyone like to join me?" The troll walked towards the kitchen.

"Splendid idea," Fergus replied. "We could all use a break."

Everyone sat at the table sipping tea, faces blank, processing all that had happened. No one spoke for quite some time.

"So now what happens? And what about my mother? Where is she?" Sam broke the silence.

"Your mother. Oh Sam. I was so focused on Ornoth, I forgot. If the curse has been broken, and the brambles are gone, your mother... She is in great danger," Fergus said with alarm. "We must go to her now. Steffan, is there a potion for this? Is there a way to keep her safe?"

Steffan dropped his head. "Fergus, I'm afraid that the Black Thatcher must have been giving her the bramble juice, the elixir of immortality. Without it, she can't live for long."

Sam gasped, "You mean my mother is going to die?"
Steffan gave the bad news. "I'm sorry Sam. When the Black Thatcher was killed, it lifted all his curses. Most likely everything in the castle has been subject to a curse or enchantment. The only way we will know for sure is to go to the castle. We must go now and hope your mother is still alive."

Fergus spoke up, "I will fly ahead. Steffan, the carriage and horses are still here. You can bring the children with you to the castle. We must hurry." Fergus hopped out the door and jumped into the air. "I will meet you there," said the crow, his voice fading in the distance.

Ornoth stood on the porch waving to the group leaving for the castle. "I will await your safe return. Please send a message if you need me for anything."

CHAPTER TWENTY-FIVE

The castle loomed in the distance as the carriage bounced and rumbled along the rock scattered dirt road. Sam sat close to Annie, holding her hand and hoping that his mother was safe. So much had happened.

"Annie, I am so frightened. I was so close to being with my mother again and she may already be dead," shouted Sam as he tried to be heard over the thundering sound of the horses. He wished he could fly to the castle, like Fergus did.

"Sam, you must have faith. There is still hope." Annie leaned closer to the boy.

"I think we are almost there. Look." Sam pointed to the steep towers and the large wooden door leading into the castle.

The door swung open, Fergus pushing from the other side. "That door was much heavier than I anticipated. I think my wing is bent." Fergus held out his wing, now with a distinct kink.

"We must get to Sam's mother. Hurry. Do you remember where she was being held?" Steffan asked.

"This way." Fergus hopped down the right corridor. "In here."

Sam unbolted the door, unsure what he would find. Slumped in the chair was his mother, her eyes closed and her body still. "Mama. Mama," Sam shouted. There was no response. He had hoped she would still be alive.

"Martha. Can you hear me?" Fergus leaned over the still woman.

"Sammy," sounded a weak voice. "Sammy." Already the woman had aged, her hair gray and her skin withered.

Relieved, Sam yelled, "Mama, you're alive. Yes. It's me, Sammy. Please open your eyes. You are safe now. The Black

Thatcher has been killed." He grabbed her hand and squeezed it tight.

Slowly, the woman opened her eyes. "Who…"

"Mama, I've brought Steffan, the true King," announced Sam.

Steffan leaned over the woman. "You have a wonderful son here. He has gone through many challenges to find you. I know you have been held captive for a long time."

The woman seemed to be regaining strength. "Yes. I cannot even count how many years I have been here. I never thought I would see my son again and here he is, right before my eyes." Martha's eyes filled with tears. "My Sammy." She reached out her arms.

Sam hugged his mother and felt her heartbeat next to his. He was so happy that she was alive and speaking to him. "Mama. I will never leave you again." Sam's sobs were happy ones.

"Fergus - go look in the cellar and see if there is any elixir left. We may be able to keep Martha alive, for a little while at least," the King whispered to the crow.

"Yes Steffan. I know exactly where the cellar is. I passed it when they put me in the dungeon." Fergus hurried off.

"Sam. Tell me again how you ended up here. You died many years ago. You were eleven then. How old are you now?" the woman asked her son.

"I am still eleven. I died but no one ever came for me. There were no angels. I thought maybe you would find me once you died. I waited for you for so long, but you never came, and I never got any older. I wasn't alive but I wasn't in heaven either." Sam told his mother all about the forest in Willow Glen, about how he met Annie and Sadie, how they tumbled through the trunk and how they ended up at Ornoth's cabin.

"Oh, Sammy. You must've been so lonely. I am so sorry. The last thing I remembered was the church." Sam's mother shared her memories. "I was so sad losing you."

"Mama, don't talk. Save your strength," Sam pleaded with the rapidly aging woman.

"Here, I found some elixir." Fergus bounded in and held a glass up to the dry mouth of the now, very old woman.

"No. I do not want to drink that vile drink." Martha pushed the glass away.

"But it will reverse the aging. It will give you more time with your son," Fergus explained.

"I have far outlived my time. It need to go. Sammy? Come closer." The weak woman reached out for her son.

"Mama, you can't leave now. Please drink the juice," Sam begged. He was so afraid. "Mama, please."

"I cannot stay. I have no more strength. This is not where I belong. I will wait for you in heaven. I promise." Martha heaved a sigh and fell limp.

"Mama. Mama." Sam threw himself across his mother's lifeless body. He no longer felt her heartbeat.

"She's gone. She made her own choice." King Steffan reached for the boy who was now shaking with grief.

"If she's gone, I want to go too. Let me die. I want to be with my mother," Sam wailed, his loud sobs echoing through the cell.

"Sam, you don't have to go yet. You're alive now. Why do you want to be dead?" Annie pleaded with the boy.

Sam wanted them all to leave. He wanted to be alone with his mother. Maybe he could will himself dead.

§§§

Annie turned to Steffan. "What can be done? Is there a way Sam could be with his mother?" Annie asked.

The King pulled Sam away from Martha's form, handing the boy to Fergus. Steffan gently picked up the woman and carried her still body out of the castle, placing her gently in the carriage. "Fergus, bring Sam. I have an idea." He waited for Fergus, then helped Sam up onto the seat. The boy was still crying, begging to die so that he could be with his mother. "Let's go back to the cottage. I know where the trunk is."

Annie climbed into the coach and sat opposite her friend. "Sam, I am so sorry. I never imagined this is how things would end up." Annie tried to hug Sam, but he pushed her away. She knew he was upset but nothing she did consoled him.

"You don't know what sorry is. I'm sorry I ever met you. I'm sorry I ever came here. I should've stayed in the forest. I should've stayed dead." Sam's grief had turned to anger.

"You don't mean that. You would've never found your mother if we hadn't come here," said Annie as she tried to reason with Sam. If she could make him understand how much Mrs. Sullivan had suffered.

"We killed her. She was alive. She could've lived forever." The boy's tears continued falling.

"Sam, she wasn't living. She was being held captive by a terrible creature. She was being forced to drink juice made from the lives of the forest creatures. I'm sure had she known, she would've been horrified," Annie remarked, trying to imagine how Sam's mother must've felt being forced to drink the bramble wine.

"But Annie, how can I be alive, and she is now dead? It isn't fair." Sam's sobs were inconsolable.

"Look." Annie pointed out the window. The forest had come alive. There were animals everywhere. Rabbits, squirrels, foxes, and deer hopped and ran freely through the woods. It made Annie happy to see them finally freed from the Black Thatcher's curse.

"Up ahead. It's not too much farther." The King steered the horses towards Ornoth's cabin. "There. I believe the trunk is near that tree." The King pulled the carriage alongside a large fir tree. "Over there. I see it."

Annie and Sam climbed out of the coach. Steffan picked up Martha's body and lifted her gently, placing her inside the leather trunk. Her lifeless body now appeared over a hundred years old, her skin wrinkled and her hair white. "Sam, are you sure you want to be with your mother?" King Steffan asked.

"Yes, I am sure. I was dead before and at least this time I know how to find my mother." Sam moved towards the trunk.

The King knelt down and placed his hands on the young boy's shoulders. "Taking one's life is a serious thing. But in this case, I believe the fairies enabled you to be alive again. I believe they helped you and Annie come here so that you could find your mother. I also believe that it is time for the fairies to help you to travel to the realm in between blinks, a place that you should've gone many years ago. There, you and your mother can be together again. Fergus, I think it's time you summon the fairies," the King directed his comment to the sobbing crow.

"Yes, of course." Fergus regained his composure and prepared for the summoning. He swirled around and around, chanting magical words. A cloud of sparkling lights surrounded the large bird. One by one the lights took shape and soon there were at least fifty fairies flittering before the dancing bird.

"You have summoned us? How can we help?" a fairy asked.

Fergus pointed towards the trunk. "This is Martha. She has died and needs to be taken to the afterworld realm. She was bewitched and was being held captive by the Black Thatcher," Fergus explained. "And this is Sam. He is Martha's son and he wants to be with his mother."

"But he is very much alive," the fairy replied. "We can't kill him."

"But he was dead and was only alive as the result of magic. Magic from this trunk, actually." Fergus pointed to the brown crate.

"Oh, I know of this trunk. It travels between time. We see it, then we don't see it, then we see it again." The fairy flew closer to the trunk. "It is bewitched for sure."

Sam spoke to the group of fairies. "My mother arrived here in that trunk, over a hundred years ago, and then Annie and I arrived also, but a hundred years later. I was dead but the trunk made me alive again. I don't want to be alive any longer. I want to go be wherever my mother goes."

The group of fairies gathered around the crate. One spoke up. "This is a most unusual situation but because Annie has fairy magic surrounding her, it seems likely that her enchantment has helped you get to this point."

"What do you mean?" Annie asked.

"I see it in your aura. It is written there. You won't remember but when you were an infant, the fairies found you alone in the forest. You were brought into our realm and kept safe until the time when you could be returned to the human world. You were given special magic, fairy magic," the fairy explained.

"Fairy magic? You mean I'm a fairy?" Annie's face lit up. "At the orphanage, they used to tease me about having been stolen by fairies. I never thought it was true."

"You weren't stolen. You were rescued. Although you are most definitely a human, you do have fairy dust in your blood. It allows you to see and hear nature in a way most humans can't. It's why animals come up to you, unafraid. It's how fairies can speak to you in your dreams." The fairy's wings unfolded. "Now that you are older, you will notice the magic diminishing, unless of course, you want it to stay."

"Oh, yes, yes. Please allow it to stay." Annie was excited at the revelation. "Why wasn't I ever told of this fairy magic?"

"There is a time and place for everything. You have now seen the way we work and can now understand how important it is for you to safeguard your secret. Use your abilities wisely and they will serve you well," the fairy explained. "Very well then. It is now time to help Sam and his mother reach the afterworld." The fairy flew off to join the others.

So many things now made sense to the young girl. If only she had known. "If I ever get back home again, I will do wonderful things," said Annie, filled with hope.

The fairies turned their attention to the distraught boy. "Sam, we need you to understand. Once we perform this ceremony, it cannot be undone." The fairies all nodded in unison. "Are you sure you want us to continue?"

"Yes, I am sure." Sam joined the fairies then looked at Annie. "I'm sorry Annie. I need to do this. I hope you find your way home. If it wasn't for you and your fairy magic, none of this would've happened."

Annie hugged Sam. "I understand. I will miss you, but I know how important this is to you. Please don't forget me." Annie's face was wet with tears. They had been through so much together. It saddened her that she was losing her friend but she knew it was best for Sam to be with his mother.

"Annie, I will never forget you. I hope you find your way back home, and Ornoth, how can I ever repay you? If it hadn't been for you, I would've been brambled." Sam gave Ornoth a big hug, the boy's arms barely reaching around the wide troll.

"My pleasure, young man." A tear rolled down Ornoth's face and fell from his bulbous nose.

"And Fergus, oh Fergus. Thank you so much for everything you have done for me." Sam burrowed into the crow's black feathers.

Fergus's large wings stroked the boy's head. The hug said everything.

"King Steffan, I don't feel like I know you although I know you have been here the whole time. I am so glad the curse has ended for you. Please take care of Annie." Sam bowed before the King.

The King grabbed the boy and hugged him tightly. "You are a very brave young man. It has been my pleasure to know you."

Sam turned to the group of fairies. "I guess I am ready. Will it hurt?"

"No, it won't hurt. Climb into the trunk and get as close to your mother as you can. We will do the rest." The fairies surrounded the crate, their wings buzzing.

Annie watched as Sam snuggled next to his mother. She wondered where they would end up. The fairies closed the lid.

CHAPTER TWENTY-SIX

The fairies circled the trunk and began flying in a spiral. They flew faster and faster until a column of purple light flashed through the sky. The crate rose up off the ground and spun and swirled. It turned blue, then orange, then pink, finally bursting into sparkly silver dust. The dust rose higher and higher and then made a loud pop as it disappeared completely. The fairies vanished at the same time.

"Where did they go?" Annie's eyes widened as she witnessed the fairy magic.

"They are now in the afterworld. The fairies know the way," Fergus replied. "Sam and his mother are together again in the realm in between blinks."

The King led the way into the cabin. "We still need to figure out how to get Annie home. Do you think the fairies could help her too? After all, she does have fairy dust in her blood."

Annie thought about how much had changed. Ornoth was back to his old troll self. King Steffan was back to his King self. Fergus was still Fergus. Sylvia was in the afterworld realm, maybe with Sam and his mother. The Black Thatcher was dead and all those who had been brambled were now free.

Steffan pulled out a chair at the kitchen table. "Is the tea ready?" Ornoth poured tea for all four of them. He placed a plate of biscuits on the table next to the jar of jam.

"Why do you drink so much moss tea?" Annie asked.

"You don't know?" Ornoth looked up with a puzzled look. "Curious. One day you will remember." The troll gave a big toothy grin.

"Delicious," Steffan exclaimed. "It tastes much better in this body than in yours." The King winked at his troll friend.

"How does it feel to wear all those heavy clothes?" Ornoth asked Steffan. "At least you didn't leave my body as a naked man," Ornoth chuckled.

"I must admit, your clothing felt much lighter, Ornoth. Perhaps I will adjust my wardrobe to be more troll-like than king-like." Steffan touched his thick wool coat and trousers. "These wool clothes are scratchy and I much prefer bare feet to these heavy boots."

Ornoth laughed, moss hanging from his scraggly teeth. "I don't think my clothes will fit you any longer."

"How can you all be laughing during such a sad time?" Annie glared at the three sitting at the table.

Steffan replied, "Sam is exactly where he wants to be. He is happy. Martha is again with her son. She is happy. Why shouldn't we also be happy?"

"Because Sam is gone. We won't ever see him again." Annie wanted them to feel the way she did. She missed Sam already and it had only been a short time.

"In the afterworld realm, things are not like they are here. Those there can still see us, talk to us, and be around us whenever they want," Ornoth explained.

"But how can we talk to them?" Annie asked.

"You talk, like you are doing now. You will see them in your dreams. They really aren't gone at all," Ornoth stated.

"Fergus, why are you so quiet?" Steffan looked towards his feathered friend.

"I was thinking about Sam and wishing he could've stayed here with us. I understand how Annie feels." Fergus bowed his head.

"But we need to be happy for him. He is happy where he is. I am sure of it," Steffan remarked. "Now it's Annie's turn."

"There will be time for that," Annie stated, "but now I want to enjoy the time I have with all of you."

"Come. Let's walk outside and see how the forest is doing," said Steffan.

Annie noticed animals scattering around and birds singing in the trees. She wondered if they would be able to find their homes again. "It seems so normal like everything is as it should be."

"I can only hope that all will find their families again. As for me, I wonder how old I am?" The King questioned.

"How old were you when you were cursed?" Annie asked.

"I don't remember. Perhaps it no longer matters. It does appear that I am strong and healthy, and have many years of life remaining," announced Steffan, his voice hopeful.

"Or maybe forever," Fergus replied.

"Forever? I do not have any elixir, my good friend," answered the King.

"No, but you still have the sword," said Fergus.

"The sword? Why yes, but does it have that kind of magic?" asked Steffan.

"Sylvia told me some things about the sword. She knew the enchantress who had it first. There was great magic placed in it but only the right person, the one with the purest of soul and kindest of heart, could access all its powers." Fergus scratched his beak. "From what I recall, one of those powers was immortality."

"If what you say is true, what makes you think that I am the right person?" The King asked.

"I don't know. I only know you as being part of Ornoth and how you cared for me. I know how you cared for the children. I know how you spoke of the forest beings after they'd been brambled. I can only guess that you might be the one; the one with a pure soul and kind heart." Fergus stretched out his bent wing. "Now if you had the power to straighten out my wing."

Steffan laughed. "Come here my friend." He pulled on the bent feathers. "This may hurt." A loud crack sounded.

"Oh, much better." Fergus fluffed up his feathers. "I wish I knew how to help Annie get home. Do you have any ideas, Steffan? I wish Sylvia was here. She would know."

Annie stepped through the wildflowers, her small footprints barely making a dent. She watched Fergus hop back and forth, his joy evident. Steffan stood quietly. She noticed a small orb of light appearing some distance away, coming closer and closer.

"What is that, Fergus?" Annie pointed at the orb.

"I don't know," said the crow, his eyes focused on the approaching light.

Annie watched as the orb took shape.

"Don't you recognize me?" sounded a voice. "You asked for me."

"Who are you?" Steffan did not recognize the voice.

"It's me, Sylvia. Someone asked for me. Who is asking?"

Fergus spoke up. "It was me, Sylvia. I hoped you could hear me. I am so glad you came. There is so much that has happened."

"Of course I heard you. I am closer than you know." The woman now appeared in a wispy form.

"Did you have to travel far?" Fergus asked.

"Not far at all. The afterworld is near, right next to you. The dead are still here. They barely leave at all. As a matter of fact, Martha and Sam say hello," Sylvia commented.

"You saw Martha and Sam? How are they?" Annie asked, startled.

"They are doing fine, all things considered. They just arrived. Martha is a beautiful soul, young and vibrant, and Sam is a character. I can tell they will love being on the other side of the veil."

Annie gazed at the wispy shape and could make out Sylvia's face. "You look so young," Annie commented. "You don't look dead at all."

"Death is an illusion," Sylvia explained. "The land in between blinks is much closer than you realize, perhaps the thickness of a feather."

"Sylvia, I am so glad you came. I have so many questions," said Steffan. "You must already know that the Black Thatcher is dead. Hopefully he didn't go to the realm in between blinks."

"I know about the Black Thatcher. There was great rejoicing when that happened. He is in a different place than the rest of us. It will take much time to remove the evil from his soul," Sylvia commented.

"I would imagine he would be in hell, for sure," the King shouted.

"No, no. There is no hell. But there is a place for special healing. A soul who was that evil, that selfish, that cruel, needs a lot of healing," Sylvia explained. "Every soul starts out pure, but sometimes things happen, things beyond our control. Different experiences and awful things can fracture a soul in horrible ways. It is not for us to judge, but what we do is to help the soul find its way back to its pure self. There is forgiveness that comes with that."

"How can anyone forgive the Black Thatcher for what he did?" King Steffan said with anger.

"He did horrible things. It will require a great deal of work by those in the afterworld who do the healings, to help him recover his soul. He will go through much emotional pain, great grief, and sadness," Sylvia commented with compassion. "All those he tortured will also receive special attention. They will be loved, nurtured and helped in all ways possible to restore their souls to wholeness."

Steffan shook his head. "I do not know if I can forgive that evil man."

"It takes a pure soul and a kind heart to be able to forgive." Sylvia chose her words with care.

In a flash, Steffan understood. "Of course. The sword. Thank you, Sylvia. You have reminded me of something extremely important."

"I am here whenever you need me," Sylvia replied. "Now Annie, sweet child. You must want to go home," said Sylvia, her voice full of love. "Know that Sam and his mother are fine. I have seen them, and they are very happy," Sylvia stated.

"That is wonderful news. I miss Sam already, but it brings me comfort to know he is happy." A tear ran down Annie's face.

"Oh, please don't cry sweet girl. There are many here who are watching over you." Sylvia moved closer to the young girl. "Not only do you have the fairies guiding over you, you also have loved ones."

"Loved ones? Who is watching over me?" Annie asked.

"Your parents. They are both here and always with you," Sylvia whispered.

"But my parents are in Willow Glen. At least I hope they are still alive there," Annie said with worry. "They're not dead, are they?"

"Remember how you told me you were found in the forest?" Sylvia asked.

"Yes, but…" Annie uttered.

"Those parents are here. Your mother and father. They perished when you were a baby. Something tragic happened at the lake and you were left under a tree. Their bodies were never found."

"What happened to them?" Annie tried to comprehend the story Sylvia was telling.

"That isn't important. What matters is that they have great love for you and need you to know that," Sylvia continued.

"I never imagined that I had another set of parents who loved me." Annie didn't know how to feel.

"Your parents asked the fairies to step in. You would've perished for sure, had they not. When the fairies saw hunters in the forest, they believed it was an opportunity for you to be found. They returned you to the same place under the tree so that you could be rescued," Sylvia explained.

"So, if the fairies hadn't taken me, I would've died?" Annie asked.

"Most likely, and your parents wanted you to have a nice, long life. They knew it wasn't your time so they asked the fairies to intervene." Sylvia's voice sounded like when she was alive. "The fairies took excellent care of you and bestowed on you some abilities. As you get older, you will be shown more."

"I am not sure I understand," said Annie as she struggled with the story.

"You have never been alone," Sylvia stated.

"You mean, my birth parents have been with me all this time?" Annie asked.

"Yes, Annie. They watched over you at the orphanage and they also helped find the parents who adopted you."

"I don't know what to say. This is, uh, I didn't know it worked this way," Annie commented. "I always thought I was stolen by fairies and that maybe, I wasn't even human."

"You are very human, but you are also special, indeed. The fairies enchanted you. There is more for me to tell you about them but that is for another time. Know that fairies will always be around you, and so will your birth parents." Sylvia began to fade.

"Wait. Don't go yet. Please tell me more about my parents. I need to know more," Annie begged.

"Know that your loved ones are with you always. Death does not take them away. It only takes their bodies, however their souls, the part of them who stays in your heart, is never gone. Love is what keeps them close. You can see them in your dreams." Sylvia was barely visible now.

Annie's emotions were hard to contain. "Thank you so much Sylvia. I thought I was all alone."

"You are surrounded, believe me. And you have me now too, and Martha, and Sam. You will never be alone. None of you will be alone." Sylvia slipped away until only a bright orb of white light floated midair, then vanished.

"I never…" Steffan stammered.

"Amazing," Fergus exclaimed.

"My parents. My parents are here. I can feel them." Annie rubbed her arms. "I'm tingling."

"Me too." Fergus ruffled his feathers.

"And I am too." The King felt a shiver run down his body. "I understand now what needs to be done. Sylvia gave me the answer I sought. It is clear to me what I must do." The King strode away.

CHAPTER TWENTY-SEVEN

All four of them, Annie, Steffan, Fergus, and Ornoth, went back to the cabin. Annie settled into the pillow on the sofa, still buzzing from the visit from Sylvia. Ornoth was sitting by the fire and Fergus was perched on his favorite chair. Steffan was in the kitchen looking for something to eat. Annie was looking through Ornoth's books, hoping to find something that might help her know how to get back home.

"Ornoth, I found a book about the world. Look. There are maps inside." Annie flipped through the pages.

"What is all that blue?" Fergus asked.

"Those are the oceans, you silly crow." Annie enjoyed spending time with Fergus. "Here is Asia and here is South Africa. Over here is South America and this is England."

Fergus scratched his head. "I know not of any of those places. Where might this forest be?"

"You have never told me the name of the forest," Annie stated.

"It has no name other than forest," said Fergus scratching his head.

"It must have a name. How do you know where you are if you can't find it on a map?" Annie looked at Fergus with a serious look on her face.

"How do I know that this map is real?" Fergus asked.

"It just is. Explorers discovered all these places and then drew them on a map," Annie said. "They must've asked the people the names of where they lived."

"Maybe Steffan knows what the forest is called," Fergus shouted out. "Steffan, what is the name of your Kingdom?"

"My Kingdom? Hmmm. I have only called it my Kingdom," Steffan replied.

"You're no help," Annie commented then shrugged. She continued looking through the books. She found stories and poems, strange journals with odd symbols, and a variety of writings on plays, music, and art. Shaking her head, "All these books and Fergus doesn't even know where he lives."

Steffan entered the room, his hands full of biscuits. "I don't think it ever had a name. We always called it the forest, the castle and the kingdom. Why would I never have known the name? That is odd. Come to think of it, I really don't even remember my father, or my grandfather, or even my mother. I assumed they were here before me."

"So, what do you remember?" Annie was even more curious, now.

"I remember riding a horse. I was around eleven or twelve, about the same age as you, I think. I remember servants and guards. There was a cook, a very good cook. She would prepare the best stew in the whole land." Steffan smiled as the memory surfaced.

"And this land. What was it called?" Annie again asked.

"The forest, oh fandaddle. Why can't I remember that?" The King sounded frustrated.

"Your mother. What did she look like?" Annie asked another question.

"She was, uh, she wore, hmmm. Her hair was... I don't remember. People would say the Queen this or the Queen that. The Queen must've been my mother. Why can't I remember her?" Steffan was really upset now. "I think I am done with these questions. Come Fergus. I could use your help." The King left with Fergus close behind.

Annie hadn't meant to upset Steffan. Still, she wanted to know where she was so she could figure out how far away Willow Glen might be. Books lay scattered across the table as Annie poured over every map she could find. She hoped someone may have mentioned Willow Glen, yet all she found were strange recipes, chants, incantations, and symbols. Sometimes the pages would have pressed flowers or herbs smashed between them. Annie liked to hold the books to her nose and smell the scents. She felt drawn to one journal, in particular. It had a red leather binding and the pages were bulging out. It was tied with twine so the contents could not fall out. Annie pulled it from the shelf and carefully freed the pages from their wraps.

"What might I find inside you?" Annie spoke as she opened the book.

"That is for you to discover," sounded a voice.

"Who said that?" the young girl inquired.

"It is me, the Book of Secrets." The book shook a little.

"Books can't speak." Annie stared down at the embellished pages.

"I hold the answers that you seek. You need only look," the book responded.

"I suppose if I am in a land where there is a talking crow, it shouldn't surprise me that there could be talking books," Annie commented. "I do have some questions though."

"Please ask." The pages began to flutter.

"I would like to know what the name of the forest is, the one that surrounds the castle?" Annie hoped the book knew the answer.

The book replied, "The forest has no name. It is not necessary."

"Then how might I know where I am?" Annie asked.

The book commented, "You are right where you are."

"That is no answer. I must know the place so I can find it on the map." Annie was getting upset.

"It is not on a map." The book stood on end.

"Why not? It is a place and places should be mentioned on maps." Annie crossed her arms, frustrated. This book was being difficult and the answers were all in riddles.

"A place is where you are, and where you are is where your thoughts are. It isn't here or there, it's everywhere," the worn pages uttered.

"You are no help at all. I thought you said you would have the answers that I was seeking." Annie wanted to throw the book to the ground. She was getting nowhere.

"I have given you the answers," the book snapped.

"You aren't telling me what I need to know," Annie shouted back.

"You need only to know that you are here, there and everywhere." The journal closed shut.

Annie retied the book with the twine and placed it back on the shelf. Her eyes were heavy, so she sat down at the table and placed her head down. Her thoughts drifted to Sam, then to home, and then to Sadie. Oh how she missed Sadie. She could see her dog, running and jumping. She remembered playing fetch with her Sadie, watching her jump into the water and then shaking it all off. "Sadie, I wish that I could be home with you." The girl's thoughts grew fuzzy as she fell into a deep sleep.

CHAPTER TWENTY-EIGHT

"Annie, Annie, wake up?" the muffled voices sounded in the distance. "What more can we do?"

Annie heard the voices somewhere in her mind. They were so far away, she figured they must be coming from another room. She ignored them and tried to focus on the images inside her head. Maybe she was dreaming. She saw her dog, Sadie. Her parents were there too. They were having a picnic, throwing a stick for Sadie to fetch. "Can you see me? I'm here, here in this cabin," Annie's thoughts shouted. Her parents stopped for a moment, looked around but then went back to throwing the stick. "Please, come get me, please," Annie repeated her request. Her voice sounded funny. Why couldn't they hear her?

"Annie, please wake up. Please, we are worried about you." Annie again heard the muffled voices.

Crash! Something fell to the ground. Suddenly, Annie felt water splashed on her face. "What are you doing?" Annie sat up, her face soaking wet.

"Oh, thank goodness. She is awake," said Steffan, relieved. "Annie, we have been so worried."

"Worried? But why?" Annie asked, shaking her head a little.

"You've been asleep for days. We found you on the floor. We couldn't wake you so brought you here, to Ornoth's bed. Ornoth, Fergus and I have been taking turns sitting by you, afraid that you were dying." The King's voice saddened. "Here, you must drink some water." Steffan offered Annie some sips from a goblet. "Please, a little more." The drowsy girl drank a few more sips.

"I was dreaming. I saw Mama and Papa and my dog Sadie. They were having a picnic. I tried calling out to them, but they couldn't hear me. At first, I thought they could. They looked around like they had heard me shout. It made me feel so homesick. Oh Steffan, Fergus, I want to go home. I must go home. Isn't there some way that you can help me?" Annie begged, describing the vision she had seen. It seemed so real.

"You will feel better after you have something to eat," Fergus commented. "I know you believe the maps hold the secret to you returning back to your home. I think I have another idea though."

"You do? Please tell me." Annie's hope rose.

"Remember when you told us about Phillip, the pixie you met in the cave?" Fergus asked.

"Oh yes. I met Phillip in Willow Glen. It was a crystal from his cave that allowed me to see Sam, even though Sam was a ghost," Annie recalled.

"And didn't you also see Phillip here, in our land? Wasn't he who meshed you and sent you to see Sylvia?" Fergus helped Annie remember.

"Yes, yes. He was here in this forest. He was also in Willow Glen. That's it. He knows where I live. He can help me find it," the young girl said with excitement.

"Do you still have the crystal, the one you found near your home?" Fergus asked.

"I think so." Annie felt for the stone in her pocket. "Yes, it's right here."

"We must tell the King," Fergus responded. "But first, you need to eat. Humans require food to live and you haven't eaten in days. I have prepared something you will like." Fergus waved a spoon.

"I guess I am hungry." Annie rubbed her stomach. "Why do you think I was asleep for so long? I don't remember anything except the dream I had of my parents and Sadie."

Ornoth sat in a chair near Annie. "You were reading the books from my shelves. There are many stored in the library. Some have herbs and scents from potions trapped within the pages. You must've found one that had a sleeping spell. I should've warned you," said Ornoth, his face sullen. "We weren't sure if you were ever going to wake up."

"Where did these books come from?" Annie asked.

"Before the curse, many wise ones, even sorcerers, passed through the forest. They brought with them knowledge and magic, potions, herbs, spells, and even curses. There were needs for all. They would write all they knew into the books, their own journals, and then give them to someone trustworthy when they were ready to pass on to the next world. I kept some here and Sylvia had some at her cottage," Ornoth explained.

Annie shook her head. "I must've read a bewitched one. I'm glad I'm awake now. I'm very hungry. I see some scones and moss tea. Would you all like to join me?"

"I never turn down moss tea." The King poured himself a cup.

"Neither do I." Fergus grabbed himself a cup.

"Nor I." Ornoth winked at Annie. "I think you have finally remembered why we drink moss tea."

Annie smiled. She had remembered. The moss from the forest had magical properties. She wondered if she could find this moss if she ever returned home. She looked around the table at the handsome King, the lovable troll, and the large crow. "No matter what happens, I will never forget you three. I owe you so much. Fergus, you are the smartest, bravest, kindest crow any girl could ever meet. Ornoth, at first your appearance frightened me but I have learned that it's what is on the inside that matters. You are so sweet and lovable, and I do love you very much." She placed a peck on Fergus's beak, and one on Ornoth's nose.

"What about me?" Steffan asked.

"I love you too. I hope it's allowed for me to kiss a King." Annie blushed as she kissed Steffan on the cheek.

"I will never forget you either, Miss Annie." Fergus wrapped his wing around the young girl in a big feathered hug.

"And neither will I." The King squeezed Annie's hand with a warm touch. "If I had a daughter, I would want her to be like you."

"I haven't met many humans but I am lucky to have met you. You will be in my heart, always." Annie saw tears in Ornoth's eyes.

The four became quiet as they sipped their tea and ate their scones. Another adventure awaited. Annie hoped the pixie cave was still there and that they could find Phillip. She hoped he had the answers and knew the way for her to get home. The crystal was the key. She knew it.

CHAPTER TWENTY-NINE

"Time to go. Fergus, can you fly ahead and lead the way?" Steffan asked Annie. "Do you have everything? Knapsack? Crystal?"

"Please stop worrying. I have everything. Fergus even gave me a few of his feathers in case I need to use the potion again. He told me what to do," Annie remarked. "Let me say good-bye to Ornoth. I doubt I will be seeing him again." Annie ran up to the troll who was standing on the porch, his hairy bare feet hard to miss. "I will miss you so much." Annie gave Ornoth a huge hug.

"I will miss you too. I am so glad we met. Be safe. Soon you will be home," said the troll, his voice shaky.

Annie stepped into the carriage and waved to Ornoth. "Bye. I love you."

Steffan snapped the reins. "Let's go," the king shouted to his horse.

Fergus hopped, skipped and jumped into the air; his wings spread out like a large eagle. Soaring overhead, he could easily be seen.

Annie hoped it wouldn't take long to get to the caves. She wondered if Phillip would be there and if he could help. She held her crystal in her hand as the carriage rumbled down the dirt road through the thick forest. She could see Fergus in the sky from her window, diving down as though to land.

The carriage stopped. Annie climbed out and saw that Fergus was standing in a clearing.

"It's over there," Fergus pointed.

"Yes, that's it," Annie exclaimed as she ran closer to the cave opening. "I don't think you two will fit." Annie scanned the size of Fergus and Steffan. Before anyone could stop her, Annie climbed through the hole. "I will go inside and find Phillip and bring him out here to you."

"No, wait. You can't go in there without us," the King warned, but Annie was already inside.

Annie remembered the twists and turns of the cave. She remembered the shiny crystals in the walls and the smell of the damp dirt. Holding the purple stone, she called out, "Phillip, where are you? It's me, Annie." There was no reply. "Phillip, I need your help. Please come."

A sparkling light moved closer and closer before forming into a full-size pixie. Annie was delighted that it was Phillip.

"Annie. What a surprise. What brings you here?" Phillip's voice squeaked.

"The Black Thatcher is dead. I have been staying with Steffan, er, I mean Ornoth and Fergus." Annie had so much to tell the pixie.

"I knew about the Black Thatcher. It was wonderful to have so many pixies arrive home, those we had thought were lost forever. There was great rejoicing. I thought you and Sam would be home by now. Wasn't Sylvia able to help get you home?" Phillip asked.

"Haven't you heard about Sylvia?" Annie asked.

"No. Has something happened?" Phillip said with concern.
"Sylvia is dead. The Black Thatcher's curse killed her." Annie relayed the bad news.

"Oh no! How can that be? She was one of the most powerful spellbinders around," said Phillip, appearing shocked.

"She let the sunlight hit her and it killed her. We were rescued by Fergus and went back to Ornoth's cabin." Annie explained what had happened.

"I am so sorry, Annie. I had hoped this would've had a happier ending." Phillip's face filled with sadness.

"It did for Sam. He found his mother at the castle. She was a prisoner of the Black Thatcher until Ornoth killed him. Because the Black Thatcher's death ended the curse, Sam's mother started to die and we couldn't save her. Sam decided to die along with her. They were both taken by the fairies." Annie choked up as she told the story.

"I see, the land in between blinks," Phillip stated.

"I keep hearing about this land in between blinks. Is it heaven?" Annie was confused.

"It is and so much more. It is also where dreams live and where imagination lives. Even here - this forest, this cave, this land; it is all in between blinks," Phillip commented.

"I don't understand. You mean it isn't real?" Annie questioned the pixie.

"It is very real, but in a different way." Phillip hoped the young girl understood.

"Confusing. I really do not understand. It all sounds so peculiar," Annie commented. She wondered if maybe there wasn't even a real heaven.

"I am sorry that I won't get a chance to see Sam but how are Ornoth and Fergus?" Phillip asked.

Annie winced at the mention of Ornoth's name. She wondered how she was going to explain Steffan. "They are fine and right outside. They couldn't fit inside the cave entrance. Would you like to go see them?" Annie turned to leave.

"I can do better than that." Phillip snapped his fingers and in an instant, Fergus and Steffan were now standing alongside Annie.

"Wha, how did tha…" Steffan twirled around.

"It's much bigger in here than I imagined." Fergus looked around. "Ah, Phillip. So nice to see you again."

"Good day, my friend. Annie was telling me about everything that's happened. But where is Ornoth? And who is this human?" Phillip gazed at the stranger, suspiciously.

"Phillip, meet King Steffan, the true King. He killed the Black Thatcher and regained his rightful place as ruler of this kingdom," announced Annie.

"I thought Ornoth killed the Black Thatcher," said the pixie.

"I did but this is going to be hard to explain," Steffan spoke up. "Phillip, it's me, Ornoth."

"How can that be? You look nothing like a troll," Phillip stated.

"A curse. The Black Thatcher had cursed me years ago and turned me into a troll. I never told anyone, mostly because I didn't remember. The Black Thatcher didn't know that the sword he gave me, the one he thought was holding the curse on me, was also bewitched by a powerful sorceress. Her spell made it possible for me to use the sword against the evil lord. I severed his head. It was most unpleasant," stated Steffan.

"So, you were a troll that turned into the King?" Phillip asked.

"I have always been the King, but disguised as a troll. Fergus didn't even know." Steffan patted the crow on the head. "And Ornoth, the troll you know as Ornoth, is still fine. I was sharing his body. Thankfully, when I was released from the curse, I was able to remove myself without hurting him at all."

"Thank goodness. So Ornoth still lives?" Phillip asked hopefully.

"Yes. He is fine. He is back at his cabin if you'd like to visit. The forest is safe now," Steffan explained.

"The reason we are here today is because Steffan had an idea. We hope that you will be able to help," Fergus interrupted.

"I would be most pleased to help in any way I can. But first, let me say thank you, King Steffan, for removing the Black Thatcher from our lands. We have been trapped within our caves for so long now. Yes, we have lost many pixies to the brambles, but many have also returned to us. Families are being reunited and it is a most wonderful thing to see," said Phillip. "Is it now safe to leave our cave?"

"I assure you, it is safe," Steffan announced.

Phillip turned to Annie, "Why are you here?"

"This crystal. I told you about it before, about the time I met you near Willow Glen. I found it outside your cave, this cave," Annie remarked.

"I still don't remember you, other than when Fergus brought you and Sam here," the pixie commented.

"Then where did I get this crystal if it wasn't from this cave?" The girl showed the crystal to Phillip.

"That looks like one of our crystals. Tell me again how you found it?" Phillip examined the purple stone.

"I was with my dog Sadie. We were having a picnic and I was walking home and found the crystal on the ground. It was so beautiful and it sparkled. I put it in my pocket and that's when I saw Sam. He startled me," said Annie, recalling the memory.

"Had you met Sam before?" Phillip asked.

"No, how could I have? He was a ghost," Annie exclaimed.

"A ghost? And you had this crystal?" The pixie scratched his head then looked like he finally understood. "Now I know what happened. Don't you see? These crystals allow you to see what's in between blinks. Once found, they imprint upon you and create a strong bond. There is great magic within them."

"I don't understand," Annie remarked.

"You are traveling in between worlds. Don't you see?" Phillip tried to help Annie understand. "The crystal has great powers to show you what you cannot see. It allows you to hear what you cannot hear. And sometimes, it will allow you to know what you do not know."

"That makes no sense, no sense at all," Annie said with frustration. "It does no such thing. All that has happened is that I was able to see Sam even though he was a ghost. When we tumbled here in the trunk, that's when he became alive again."

"Was he really? Or did you only think he was?" Phillip questioned.

"You are confusing me, and it doesn't matter anyway. All I want is to go home, back to Willow Glen, back to Sadie. Can you help me?" Annie was losing her patience.

Fergus and Steffan listened to the whole story. "What do you think?" Steffan asked Fergus.

"Not sure. Sounds like a riddle to me," Fergus replied.

"Can you help Annie?" Fergus asked. "She really wants to go home, back to her family. It can't be too fun hanging around with us."

"You are fun," Annie said with a smile. "Who else could I share moss tea and scones with?"

Fergus bowed his head. "I will miss you, sweet child." He embraced the girl with his wing.

"Mush, mush, mush. So many emotions you all deal with. You should be more like pixies," Phillip remarked, then snapped his fingers.

Fergus, Steffan, and Annie were now standing next to a large pond. "Phillip, I remember this pond. I saw this before, near Willow Glen."

"Impossible. This is not anywhere near this, whatever you call it, Willow Glen. I never heard of such a place. We are here, in the forest. There are no nearby towns," Phillip said sternly.

"It doesn't matter anyway. Here, take the crystal. Do whatever you need to do to send me home." Annie handed the crystal to the pixie.

"I will do my best but once I break the crystal bond, you will no longer be able to return here," Phillip warned.

"If that's what it takes. Should I say my good-byes now?" Annie asked, her body already shaking from the anticipation of going home.

"Probably a good idea. I'm not sure how fast this will be. You might not have much time." The pixie reached in his pocket and pulled out a crystal of his own.

"Steffan, you have done so much for me and Sam. Thank you for caring for us and protecting us. I will forever see you as Ornoth but Steffan will also be there too. And Fergus, sweet Fergus. I doubt I will ever meet another crow such as you." Annie hugged the duo and kissed them each. It was so hard saying good-bye.

"Sweet child, you will be missed but never forgotten. Safe travels until we meet again," the King said solemnly.

"Annie, follow your dreams. Laugh as much as you can and love with all your heart." Fergus pulled a feather from his wing. "Please keep this. It will help you to remember me."

"Good-bye my friends. I love you." Annie placed the feather in her pocket then turned to Phillip. "Guess it's time. I sure hope this works."

"I hope so too. I have never done this before. Are you ready?"

"Yes, I'm ready," Annie replied.

Crystal shard, beam of light,
Break the bond that's holding tight.
Let this spirit soar above,
Back to her home that's filled with love.

Cancel out the crystal's charm,
Keep this soul away from harm,
Thrice I spin this shard today,
Send this child away, away.

Annie felt dizzy and tumbled and spun. The sounds were loud like wind whizzing by. She tried to open her eyes, but the force against them was too strong. She landed with a thud. "Did it work?" Annie looked around. She was still in the forest. Something was different though. The trees were spaced out more. She saw the cave and ran to the entrance; the one that she had crawled through, where she had found Phillip. "Maybe I can find him again," she thought.

The girl squeezed through the hole but this time there were no tunnels. It was all dirt, as though the cave had collapsed. She could barely get half of herself inside before hitting a wall of dark, solid soil. "Phillip, can you hear me?" Annie shouted. There was no reply.

Annie reached in her pocket for the crystal, hoping that Phillip had given it back. Instead, she found a very long crow's feather, black and shiny. "Oh, Fergus. I will never forget you." She thought of her friend.

Annie no longer had the knapsack or the vial with the potion in it. She felt again in her pocket, but the crystal was not there. She realized that Phillip must have needed to keep it to unbind her from its charm. "It worked. I must be home." The happy child jumped up and ran towards the farm, towards her mother and father, towards Sadie. "Oh, please still be there," she shouted as she ran towards home.

Arriving at the place where she first met Sam, she jumped over the log, just like before. She looked up, expecting to see Sam's face with his tousled brown hair and raggedy cap, his baggy pants with patched knees, his lonely, sad eyes. "Oh Sam, I miss you so. But I know you are with your mother. Someday I will see you again, I promise."

CHAPTER THIRTY

The closer Annie got to her home, the more she recognized. The barn came into view and Annie could see the wagon parked inside. There was Rosie, grazing in the field. "It's still there." Annie ran faster, jumping up onto the porch.

"Mama, Papa, I'm home," Annie shouted. "I'm here, I'm here!"

A large dog pushed open the door and bounded outside, then leaped into the girl's arms. "Sadie, Sadie. I have missed you so much." Annie could barely see through her tears. "Where's Mama and Papa?"

Annie hopped up the steps that led into the house. She walked through the front door and saw her mother in the kitchen and her father reading the newspaper. "Mama, Papa, I'm home. I'm home. I am so happy to see you." Annie ran to each one and hugged them with all her might. "I love you so much," Annie sobbed.

Mrs. Harper gave Annie an odd look. "That's wonderful to hear. Now go get washed up for supper."

"But aren't you happy to see me? Didn't you miss me?" Annie was confused. Why weren't they happier to see her? After all she'd been through, why weren't they more excited?

"We are always happy to see you. But it's not like you were gone very long. We saw you this morning," Mrs. Harper commented.

"If you weren't home by dusk, I would've gone back to town to find you. I figured you got distracted, on your walk home. I know how you like to adventure," Mr. Harper explained.

"But Papa, I went to the church but you didn't see me. I went to the storage room and fell into a trunk with Sam and we landed in a forest. There was a troll and a talking crow and ..." Annie tried to explain.

"Sam, your imaginary friend? That is some story. Hope you two enjoyed your walk home. At least I don't have to make another trip into town," Mr. Harper replied.

"We love your imagination, sweetheart. You should write it all down. It would make a wonderful story. Perhaps you could also have a book in the library," Mrs. Harper commented.

Annie went upstairs to her room. Everything was the same as when she'd left it. Could it be that she was gone for only a day? And what about Sam? She sat on her bed and stared at her radio, the same radio that Sam had listened to. "Sam, I wish you were here. I know you're with your mother, but I wish you were here."

"I am here." Annie heard a voice. "Could it be?" She looked around for her friend. "I hear you but where are you?" Annie asked.

"Right here. I'm standing right next to you. Don't you feel me touching your arm?" The voice sounded louder but it wasn't in her ears, it was in her head.

"Sam, I sense you. Are you really here?" Annie's skin tingled.

"Of course, I am. Don't you understand? There is another world, a world in between blinks. It's where everyone and everything is," the voice explained. "I know you can no longer see me like I can see you. Your world is different and some things don't work the same as here."

Annie didn't understand. How could Sam be talking to her even though he's supposed to be in heaven?

"In the afterworld realm, this world in between blinks, there are many places to go, people to meet, and things to learn," Sam continued. "It's not boring at all and the best part is that we can be around anyone in your world whenever we want. I know it's harder for you but we are only a prayer, a dream, or a thought away. The fairies even visit here."

"I think I understand now. This is what Phillip and Sylvia were trying to tell me." Annie relaxed a bit. "But can you tell me, are Ornoth, Steffan and Fergus there with you? Is their forest still there, and the cabin?"

"They are all here until they are somewhere else. The forest was real because you were there. That's what made it real. I don't know how to explain it better," said Sam.

"Is there a way I can see you?" Annie asked.

"Of course, that's easy," Sam replied.

"How? Do I need to find another crystal? What do I need to do?" Annie's questions flew.

"Close your eyes." Annie recognized Sam's voice.

"Alright. My eyes are closed," Annie replied.

"Think of me. Do you see me?" Sam spoke clearly.

"Of course, I see you. You're in my memory," Annie remarked.

"See how easy that was?" Sam laughed.

"But that's not what I meant. How do I see you with my eyes?" Annie asked.

"Do you need to see me with your eyes to know I'm here?" Sam sounded serious.

"I guess not." The girl became still. "So much had happened. Did I change?"

"Every experience changes us in some way," Sam said. "You now know that many things can happen in between blinks. For instance, I was a ghost. Yes, that really happened, although I found out I could've come here when I died, if I'd wanted. I guess I was supposed to wait until I met you so I could rescue my mom. You helped me find her and now we are together here."

Annie was beginning to understand.

"Even though you and I went through a lot to rescue my mother, know that now, your life is about you. You live in a wonderful home with a loving family. Oh, that reminds me, I have a message for you. Actually, just listen," said Sam.

"Hi, sweetheart. This is your mother." Annie heard a woman's voice inside her head and her head felt buzzy.

"And this is your father." Annie now heard a man's voice, but not through her ears.

"My birthparents?" Annie asked.

"Yes, sweet girl. We are here and have met Sam and his mother. They are delightful. Please know that we are always near you. Although we had to leave you so soon, the parents you have now, they are so special. There is more than enough love to go around. Know that we are only a blink away."

"I'm sorry I never got to know you. How can I talk to you?" Annie asked.

"We already can hear you - in your dreams and your thoughts," Annie's birth mother explained.

"You hear everything I think?" Annie wasn't sure she liked that.

"We try not to intrude but if you need us, we are only a thought away. We can send help, in our own special way," Annie's birthfather added.

Annie remembered the dream. "I believe I already know how to do that. I remember a dream, a very vivid dream where my parents and Sadie, and …" Annie suddenly remembered. "I need to go. Thank you for everything."

Annie quickly changed her clothes, washed her hands and face and ran downstairs. She hugged each of her parents and knelt to hug Sadie. "I have so much to tell you all but maybe I will write it all down, like a story."

"That is a wonderful idea." Annie's mother grabbed a bowl of mashed potatoes. "I made these special for you. I know how much you love potatoes."

Annie sat down for supper. "How could it get better than this?" She felt the shiny, black feather in her pocket.

THE END

www.ingramcontent.com/pod-product-compliance
Lightning Source LLC
Chambersburg PA
CBHW072112170626
46813CB00004B/1515